TATTOO

(a *Take It Off* novel)

A tattoo gets them in trouble… He will get them out.

After years of cultivating an undercover identity, Brody West is finally off the case and free to get a life of his own. All that time spent in the company of criminals and killers left him a little jaded… and with an identity crisis. He isn't sure who he is anymore, or who he wants to be.

To give him time to think, he takes a few days off from work to go fishing. On his way out of town he makes a routine stop at the bank and finds himself flirting with the girl behind the counter.

But his flirtation is cut short when criminals burst into the bank and shoot her right before his eyes.

In attempt to administer first aid, Brody reveals a tattoo on his back. A mark that will drag him and the girl into the kind of situation he was trying to get away from. But he can't walk away because he's the only thing capable of keeping Taylor alive and bringing down the guys who shot her—guys who are seriously dangerous criminals.

Praise for the **Take It Off** series

TATTOO

Take It Off Series

CAMBRIA HEBERT

Published by: Cambria Hebert Books, LLC

Your key to escape

http://www.cambriahebert.com

Interior design and typesetting by Sharon Kay
Cover design by MAE I DESIGN
Edited by Cassie McCown
Copyright 2014 by Cambria Hebert

ISBN: 978-1-938857-43-0

DEDICATION

To everyone who has a tattoo or loves someone who does.

TATTOO

"Many individuals have, like uncut diamonds, shining qualities beneath a rough exterior."
—Juvenal

PROLOGUE

Taylor

"This is 9-1-1. Please state your emergency."

The voice on the other end of the line was calm and cool, no indication at all that whoever they were would be bothered by the panic that surely waited on the other end of line.

On my end of the line.

But I didn't speak. I couldn't. I was scared, I was shaking… and I was afraid they would hear me.

"9-1-1, please state your emergency," the voice said again.

If I just sat here, if I just put the phone down where no one would see, could I be traced? Would the operator know to send help to this address? I was using my cell phone. Could a cell phone be traced like that?

My stomach churned because I honestly didn't know.

How stupid could I be? How could I have never taken the time to learn this? How could I be crouching here, under my counter, with sweat dampening my silk shirt and prayer whispering from my lips?

"I said down on the floor, now!" an angry voice demanded.

The cries and screams of people behind me echoed through my head. The sound bounced around in my brain, refusing to fade away and threatening to take what little bit of grip I had on my sanity.

I couldn't just sit here.

I couldn't just watch my life flash before my eyes. I couldn't just let this happen.

I had to *do* something.

"I'm at Shaw Trust on Sunderland Avenue," I whispered. "There is a bank robbery in progress."

"Are you inside the bank, ma'am?" the dispatcher asked. I could hear her fingers flying over her keyboard and I prayed that meant she was sending help.

"Yes," I whispered, clutching the phone.

One of the robbers was yelling at Brandy, one of my fellow tellers, to open the safe, and she was crying loudly.

"How many intruders are in the bank?"

I wasn't sure. They charged inside in a flurry of furious movement, and I ducked low, hiding myself behind my counter. "Too many," I breathed out.

"I'm dispatching several units to the scene, ma'am," the operator informed me.

My stomach twisted painfully as the man continued to shout at Brandy. He was threatening her now and it seemed to make her more hysterical. Anger burned up through my esophagus. Anger at the robbers, anger at the woman on the other end of the phone. How could she be so calm? Did she not hear the commotion going on in the background? Did she not know that our lives were in danger?

A shot rang out and Brandy screamed. I peeked out to see plaster from the ceiling rain down over Brandy's head. She threw her arms up around her for protection, and the man with the gun—the man who shot into the ceiling—grabbed her by the back of her head and slammed her into the safe. "Open it!" he roared.

"Ma'am, were those shots fired?" the operator asked.

"Yes," I hissed, my voice shaky. "Please hurry."

I could hear the people from the lobby sobbing, and my thoughts went immediately to the man just on the other side of my counter. I didn't know him, but the thought of him being hurt made my stomach churn even more.

"What the hell is this?" someone snarled above me, and I quivered.

The phone was snatched away from my ear and I whimpered as a man in tattered jeans, with a wide chest and a very lethal-looking gun in his hand, snarled at me. He pressed the phone to his ear and I could hear the voice of the operator asking me if I was all right.

Yeah, *now* she was concerned.

With a loud roar, he threw the phone down onto the shiny tile floor and it broke apart, shattering instantly. The sound of scattering pieces was nearly as loud as the gunshot just moments before.

"We got a snitch!" he yelled, reaching down. I pressed myself against the back of the counter until I felt the wood dig into the bones in my back. I slapped away his hands, but really it was useless. He outweighed me by at least fifty pounds. And he had a gun. My greatest weapon at the moment was my fingernails.

His hands were rough as he grabbed my wrist, twisting the flesh covering the bone and wrenching me out of my hiding spot. I cried out when he jerked my arm around my back, pulling so forcefully that it felt as if my shoulder were dislocated from its socket.

I didn't have time to really assess if it was or not because he jammed the nozzle of the gun into my throat. I could feel my hammering pulse thump rapidly against the cold, hard metal of the weapon.

"You call the police, bitch?" he whispered in my ear. Little dots of spit from his putrid mouth sprayed the side of my head.

I didn't say anything because my answer would only make things worse.

The heavy footfalls of someone approaching from behind made me even more nervous, and I whispered another prayer in the back of my mind. We spun, and I was sandwiched between the guy threatening me with a gun and another thief staring at me with angry dark eyes.

"You called the cops?" He said it like it was hard to believe.

"Last time I checked, robbing a bank and holding a gun on a person was a crime," I said, knowing I shouldn't, but not being able to keep the words in. I was scared, but I was also very angry.

He smacked me across the face. Hard.

His palm literally slammed into the side of my face, making my entire head fly sideways and right into the gun at my neck. The hard steel was unforgiving and it jammed into my flesh, making me cry out.

That was going to leave a mark.

[4]

"Hey," said a rough voice from off to the side. "I thought you were here for the money and not to hit women."

Part of me wanted to thank the man behind my counter for trying to defend me; the other part of me was horrified he would be punished.

Just as I feared, the man who slapped me leveled his gun at him. What was his name again? I tried to remember what it said on his ID when he showed it to me to make his withdrawal, but it was hard to think when half your face was stinging fiercely and the other half was being threatened with a bullet.

This was the worst day in the history of bad days.

"Hey! We came here for the cash!" another man behind us yelled.

I was shoved roughly forward. "Open the safe."

I wasn't going to open that safe.

I glanced at Brandy, who was huddled against the wall, crying. She didn't appear to be physically harmed, and I breathed a sigh of relief.

"I said open it!" He yanked the gun away from my neck, but I couldn't enjoy the safety because he slapped his large, sweaty palm in between my shoulder blades and thrust me forward so forcefully that I slammed into the metal door of the safe and bounced back, falling onto my ass on the floor.

A thud echoed behind me as I was pulled to my feet. He placed the gun between my shoulder blades, holding it there and directing me until I was standing right in front of the large keypad that opens the safe.

"I don't know the combination." I lied.

"Then you better hope you're physic because you got exactly ten seconds to open that vault before I shoot you."

Well, if that wasn't motivation, I don't know what was.

On shaking knees, I stepped forward, pressing a number on the pad. Then I pressed a couple more. When I hit the release button, nothing happened. But I didn't expect it to. I just wanted it to look like I was trying to open it. I wasn't opening it.

"See," I said, my voice trembling. "I don't know."

I heard the distinct sound of sirens and screeching tires and gave a sigh of relief. The cops were here!

Of course, I barely had time to celebrate because the thieves did the one thing that had the power to make me reconsider opening that safe.

Brandy was snatched off the floor and a gun was pressed to her head.

"So help me, God, if you don't open that shit right now, I will splatter her brains all over the wall."

Brandy started screaming and shaking. The man looked at me intently like he couldn't hear her pleas. His eyes were empty inside, completely devoid of any kind of feeling. It was like he had some weird ability to shut off his emotions.

It made me wonder if he was a vampire.

I shook my head, telling myself that thinking about vampires was a sign I was cracking under pressure.

"I'll open it." I promised. Risking my life for the bank was one thing, but risking someone else's life for the bank was an entirely different entity.

After a few punches to the keypad, the lock clicked free and my stomach clenched. Someone twisted a hand in my hair from behind and pulled, practically ripping the strands from my scalp. I was tossed onto the floor, landing in a heap next to Brandy, who was still crying.

I backed up, wrapping an arm around her shoulder, as three men walked into the safe, the sounds of opening duffle bags like a stab to my heart.

"Thank you," Brandy whispered, and I turned my face up to look into her red-rimmed, bloodshot brown eyes.

"No money is worth anyone's life," I whispered back.

The voice of who I assumed was a police officer boomed through the air, so loud that it came through the walls of the bank for all of us to hear. "The bank is surrounded. Release the hostages immediately," he demanded over an intercom.

Laughter floated out of the vault, and I figured that meant they didn't plan on letting us walk out of here. Silly me, I thought police presence would actually deter the robbers.

A large black duffle bag was tossed out of the vault, landing a few feet away. Crisp green bills were poking out of the top. Another one followed.

"Yo! Hurry up!" the guy guarding the door yelled to his friends, waiving around a rather large gun. He turned toward the vault, disregarding the people cowering on the floor.

One of the women lying behind him jumped up and made a run for it, right toward the exit. The gunman turned and fired off a shot, catching her in the leg. She fell onto the floor with a high-pitched scream.

I watched in morbid fascination as a puddle of dark red formed around her.

People in the bank were sobbing openly now. Some of them were pleading for their lives.

I heard someone outside yell, "Shots fired!"

My eyes traveled around the room, seeking out the man whose name I couldn't remember. Our eyes locked for one long second. It was like we were the only two people in the room. He wasn't crying or begging for his life. He wasn't sweating or looking for a way to save his ass.

He was standing there, in the center of the room, calm and strong, like this situation wasn't that big of a deal. He made me feel better, more in control.

Another duffle flew out of the vault and one of the men stepped out. There had to be millions of dollars in those bags. Not only would it ruin this bank, the people who did business here, but my father as well.

My newfound strength made me brave.

I stepped in front of one of the bags, giving a level look to the men who intended to take it. "If you leave now, you might get away."

The man standing directly in front of me smirked and the smirk turned into a full-blown smile. I realized my mistake then.

I tried to entice them with freedom, with the thought of getting away unscathed. These men didn't care about that. If I had been thinking clearly, I would have realized that from the beginning. None of them were wearing ski masks or those plastic masks that looked like creepy clowns or animals. They weren't even trying to hide their faces.

Men who didn't hide their faces in a situation like this were either really desperate or really meticulous and had a fail-proof plan. They planned to be long gone before anyone could recognize their faces.

I wasn't going to stop them.

No one was.

Tattoo

The man standing in front of me raised his gun, pointing it right at me.

And then he pulled the trigger.

1

Brody

I jerked awake and forced my body to lie still and listen to the sounds going on around me. A man could tell a lot just by listening. I liked knowing what I was dealing with that day before I even got out of bed.

The only sound I heard was the hum of the air-conditioner. I sat up, pushing the blankets down to my waist and leaning against the cheap wooden headboard. It was easy to forget I was alone. It was easy to forget I was no longer working a case, that I was no longer pretending to be someone else.

I'd spent so much time with other people (mostly criminals) and not being myself that I honestly wasn't sure who I was anymore. It was the reason I was here in this little hotel room—because I didn't have a place of my own. I hadn't had a place of my own for two years now.

The prospect of starting all over again, of reinventing myself once more, was not an exciting one. It exhausted me just thinking about it. Maybe some guys could toss aside their undercover identities like yesterday's trash, but I couldn't.

I glanced at the clock beside the bed and did a double take. It was already after ten. I couldn't remember the last time I slept so late.

I couldn't remember the last time I had a day off either. But now here I was with two full weeks stretching in front of me. Empty days to fill and no alarm clock demanding I get my ass out of bed.

So what did a guy with essentially no life outside of work do when he found himself with time off? He went fishing. I tossed the covers off the bed, letting them fall partially onto the floor and not bothering to fix them. That's what maid service was for.

Scratching myself, I went into the bathroom and took a quick shower, not bothering to shave. In the corner of the room was my bag of belongings. From inside, I pulled out a pair of worn jeans, a T-shirt, and a long-sleeved, plaid flannel that I left unbuttoned and untucked.

Before heading out the door with my bag, I slid a navy baseball cap onto my head, swiveling it around backward, and palmed the keys to my beat-up Ford pickup.

It was already hot outside; the Raleigh sun and humidity was relentless almost every time of the day. After dropping off my key to the room, I pulled out of the lot and didn't look back. My fishing pole and gear was already in the back, along with the few other items I had to my name. The drive to the Emerald Isle was two and a half hours so I decided to run through a drive-thru to get some food.

After I ordered a couple breakfast sandwiches and a large coffee, I pulled through and paid, pulling out the last bit of cash I had. Guess a stop at the bank was in order as well.

Shaw Trust was located on a busy street in Raleigh, North Carolina. I had been banking with them for the last five years. I didn't have many material goods to my name, but my bank account was better for it. Well, that and never being able to spend my own money.

The inside of the bank greeted me with a blast of cold air and was just as brightly lit as the sidewalk outside. The walls in here were white and so were the glossy tile floors. I stepped through the roped-off line, lining up behind several others already waiting. Four tellers stood behind the long wooden counter, each with their own computer.

It seemed like I stood in line forever, and I grew irritated because I just wanted to get the hell out of here and onto the open road.

Finally, it was my turn and I moved down the counter toward the last window on the end. I yanked out my wallet and bankcard, then looked up.

Suddenly the amount of time I waited didn't seem like such an inconvenience. In fact, if I had known she was the person waiting for me at the end of this counter, I would have waited longer.

Her light scarlet hair was long and filled with loose curls that fell over her shoulder and down her chest. Her complexion was flawless with the flush of fresh peaches, and her lower lip was fuller than the top, making it appear as though she had a permanent pink pout.

"How can I help you today?" she asked politely, glancing up with crystal green eyes. I watched them widen slightly and rich satisfaction flowed through me.

I wasn't pretty like her, but I wasn't completely lacking in the looks department.

"Hey," I said, leaning on the counter with both my elbows. The movement brought me a little closer to her. "I need to make a withdrawal."

She glanced down at the bankcard and ID I extended between us and then back at me. I gave her a lazy smile and she cleared her throat, taking the cards. She looked them over and then her polished fingernails flew over the keyboard.

I glanced at her chest, being distracted by her nice rack, but my eyes finally found the nameplate pinned to the front of her top. *Taylor.*

"How much would you like to withdrawal?" she asked.

"Four hundred."

She input the amount without saying anything.

"So…" I said, leaning toward her again. "You come here often?"

She rolled her eyes, but a small smile played on her lips. "Just the days I feel like earning a paycheck."

I grinned. "Paychecks are overrated," I drawled. "I'm going fishing."

"Says the man with a huge bank account," she quipped. Then she winced and looked up. "I'm sorry, I shouldn't—"

I laughed. The chagrin on her face and the way her cheeks bloomed with bright pink spots was entirely amusing. "Never said I didn't work. Just said I thought it was overrated."

She relaxed when she realized I didn't give a rat's ass that she knew how much was in my account. "You should bait your hook with hot dogs. Fish love them."

She was right. Surprise rippled through me. "You can't tell me a girl like you likes to fish."

"And what," she asked, arching a red brow in my direction, "is a girl like me?" She hit a couple keys and the little dispenser to my right started flinging out cash.

"Your withdrawal is to your right," she said professionally.

I let the cash sit there. "Are you a tomboy in disguise?" I whispered conspiratorially. I enjoyed the emotion, the animation that played over her features. She was beautiful—there was no doubt—but it seemed that she also had a lot beneath that pretty exterior.

"Don't tell anyone," she whispered back, handing me a receipt. Her teeth were really white and really straight. I got this sudden craving to run my tongue along their smooth surface.

"Your secret is safe with me." I tore my eyes away to pocket the cash, not bothering to count it. Oddly, I trusted her. I never trusted anyone.

Behind me, a loud banging sound boomed through the room, and I tensed, spinning on my heel. Four guys pushed through the entrance, each of them pulling out a gun.

I couldn't even get away from this shit on vacation.

Adrenaline spiked my system and began pumping through my veins and accelerating my heart. It didn't take an idiot to guess why they were here. This was a bank and they had guns. I looked over my shoulder at Taylor, who was watching the men with wide eyes.

"Get down!" I ordered quietly. "Hide. Hide good."

The thought of her being hurt was like a foul odor that caused me to wrinkle my nose. Taylor reacted instantly, dropping down behind the counter and out of sight. I hoped she crawled somewhere that no one would think to look for her.

I turned away, unable to see if she was on the move because I didn't want to draw any attention her way.

The men were yelling and waiving the weapons around, ordering people to hit the floor. People were crying and whimpering. The security guard who looked like a rent-a-cop pulled out a handgun and held it up with shaking hands. It was clear he had no idea where to aim because there were four criminals and only one of him.

One of the men closest to him took him out in under three seconds, hitting him in a way that made the man sprawl onto the floor, the gun lying next to him, forgotten.

I reached behind me to pull out my own weapon, my hand only meeting air. I wasn't armed. I spent the last two years with a gun or weapon on me at all times. It figures the one time I didn't wear it, I got caught up in the middle of a bank heist.

"I said down on the ground!" one of the men yelled, swinging the gun around to me. I was the only one left standing.

I held up my hands like I was surrendering and dropped down, lying on my belly. From this vantage point, I looked at the gun beside the security guard. It was across the room, but if I could get to it, I might be able to take several of these assholes out before they figured out who was shooting.

"Anyone calls the cops and I will shoot to kill," one of the men said in a calm, collected voice.

The tellers didn't keep money in cash drawers in this bank. The machines beside the patrons counted out the money and delivered it almost like an ATM. I watched as one of the guys tucked away his gun and palmed a sledgehammer.

With one powerful swing, he bashed in the first machine, reaching in his arm and pulling out fistfuls of cash.

Behind the counter, I could hear the men ordering someone to open the safe, and I prayed it wasn't Taylor. The girl started crying and I knew instantly it wasn't her. I knew on instinct that Taylor wasn't the type to lose her shit in bad situations. I might not know her, but I knew how to read people and I was never wrong.

I began to inch forward, keeping my eyes trained on the man guarding the door with his gun. The other three were behind the counter, and I knew I wouldn't have to worry about them seeing me until I was already halfway to the gun.

I blocked out all the sounds in the room; I focused on the gun, on what I had to do to get there. Once the familiar feel of that weapon was in my hand, all bets were off, and I was shooting to kill.

I managed to keep my concentration. Until I heard Taylor's voice. It's funny how something I heard so little of, something I was just introduced to, could become so innately ingrained inside me. I would know her voice anywhere. It was so familiar it was almost like my own.

"Last time I checked, robbing a bank and holding a gun on a person was a crime," she said.

I shut my eyes, wishing she had kept her mouth shut. Why hadn't she gone off and crawled in a cabinet or something?

The sound of skin hitting skin set my nerves on fire. It was almost as if I stepped in a pile of red ants and they swarmed my bare skin, racing up my legs and biting into me with every chance they got. Ripples of burning pain skittered over my skin, and I ground my teeth together.

"Hey," I called, abandoning my progress toward the gun and pushing up off the ground. I knew it might get me shot, but I'd rather take a bullet than watch her get knocked around again. "I thought you were here for the money and not to hit women."

She glanced my way with fear in her eyes, and I felt the side of my jaw tick when I saw how welted her cheek already was.

The man who inflicted those welts aimed his gun at me. It crossed my mind to dare him to shoot me. It wouldn't be the first time I took a bullet, and I could use the chaos of being shot to my advantage to get the unmanned gun.

Instead, he turned his attention back to Taylor and shoved her toward the safe.

When she didn't do what he wanted immediately, he rammed her into the unforgiving metal door and she fell back on her ass. I leaped over the counter. To hell with watching a woman get beat up.

I was guilty of a lot of things in my life, but I didn't hit women.

One of the douches trying to rob the place appeared beside me and rammed the nozzle of his gun between my shoulder blades. "Take another step and I'll shoot you."

I thought about calling his bluff.

Instead, I held up my hands like I was surrendering and watched the scene play out. It was a mistake that would likely haunt me for years.

I saw the look in the robber's eyes when he decided to shoot her. I saw the momentary thrill that being in power gave him. I moved fast, spinning instantly and disarming the guy who thought he was holding me hostage.

I hit him in the head with the butt of the gun and dropped him, turning back to Taylor.

But just as I turned, a gun went off.

2

Taylor

I never really gave much thought to what it would be like to get shot. It's probably good I never wasted my time thinking about it because I never would have imagined it would be like this.

I literally felt the bullet rip into my body. I felt the heat of the metal, and the impact of the shot spurred me backward. I lost my balance and fell. I didn't even notice my body colliding hard against the floor.

White-hot pain burned through me, eclipsing all else. I didn't think. I couldn't even react. It was almost like I was paralyzed for long moments. The pain began to ebb away, and I stared up at the bright lights in the ceiling as numbness overtook my body.

I knew I should be hurting more, but I couldn't seem to summon up the amount of worry that I needed to lift my head and look.

A flurry of movement surrounded me, and the guy whose name I couldn't remember appeared over me, clutching a gun and assessing me with a tight mouth.

One of the thieves pressed a gun to his head and his eyes narrowed.

"No," I gasped, the motion hurting me, and I moaned.

"Give me the gun or I'll shoot her again," the thief told him.

I watched him debate for a long moment, and I wondered what the hell made him hesitate. But then his eyes slid back to mine. His stare reminded me of freshly brewed espresso, dark and intense. The kind of eyes that could stare right through a person.

He put the gun down and shoved it away from us.

Part of me was disappointed, but the other part of me was charmed he would do something like that in an effort to help me.

The gun held against his head was removed and the men stealing the money started moving around a bit more. I didn't pay attention to them though because his dark, intense stare leaned closer.

"Stay with me, Taylor," he said, reaching out and wrapping a hand around my upper arm. It hurt and I cried out.

"You were shot. I'm applying pressure to the large artery running inside your arm below your armpit in an attempt to slow the bleeding." He spoke calmly, like I wasn't bleeding all over the place.

"Do you feel pain anywhere else besides your arm?" he asked.

"Is that where I was shot? My arm?"

He glanced at me. "Yes, your upper arm. I don't think it hit an artery because the pressure I'm applying is slowing the blood flow."

"It hurts," I told him.

"I know, sweetheart," he murmured, letting go of me. Pain began to throb and I felt my arms and legs begin to shake. I watched as he stripped off the flannel shirt he was wearing and draped it over my torso. It was warm and I sighed because the heat was so welcome.

"What's your name?" I asked, needing to know the name of the man who was trying to help me.

"Brody," he said as he yanked off his T-shirt, pulling it right over his head.

"This might hurt," he warned and used the T-shirt to apply renewed pressure to my arm.

He had tattoos. A lot of them. In fact, his completely shredded body was covered in them. They ran over his chest, down the impressive wall of abdominals, and across his shoulders. He had a vine that wrapped all the way down one of his arms and ended just above his wrist.

It was sexy. Probably the sexiest thing I'd ever seen. So sexy that it distracted me from the bleeding gunshot wound in my arm.

He grunted, applying more pressure, and I hissed a breath between my teeth. Sweat broke out over my forehead and my body resumed shaking.

"I'm going to get you outside, to the ambulance," Brody said as I watched the way the tattoos rippled when his muscles shifted.

My vision dimmed for a second, his figure swimming before my eyes. His fingers wrapped around the underside of my chin and he held my face, staring down. "Taylor, stay with me. Look at me."

"That won't be very hard," I murmured.

He smiled.

His body was shoved from behind and he jerked forward, slamming his hands into the floor on either side of me, using himself as some sort of defense for my injured form. Brody's entire body was like a solid piece of granite caging me in, protecting me.

"Look at this," one of the men called out.

Brody swore softly and I glanced up, meeting his eyes. "Call me Slater," he whispered.

Didn't he say his name was Brody?

Several of the men (including the one who shot me) leaned over us, staring down intently at something.

"Where'd you get that tattoo?" one of the men demanded.

The muscle in Brody's jaw jumped and a sort of coldness cloaked his body. He didn't give me another look when he pushed up and around to face the question. "I earned it."

"If you earned it, then why haven't we seen you around here before?"

"Because I earned it down the coast, not here," Brody replied.

What the hell were they talking about? I was lying here bleeding, these men were trying to steal millions, and here they were taking a timeout to discuss a tattoo?

Maybe blood loss was making me delirious. Or maybe these men were world-class idiots.

"Where?" demanded the man with a gun.

"I ran with Pike's crew. Before he got busted."

"You ran with Pike?" The man seemed skeptical.

"Indirectly. I was part of his crew in supply."

"Hell-O," I said, "I'm bleeding over here."

"Hang on, Tay," Brody said over his shoulder.

"You know her?" the man demanded.

"Yeah," Brody said tersely.

"Oh shit!" the gunman said. "Did I shoot your girl?"

"Yeah, and I gotta tell you, I'm pretty pissed off about it," said Brody... or Slater (I had no idea), folding his arms over his chest. It stretched out the skin across his wide back and I was able to see the tattoo that everyone was so worked up about.

It was circular, probably the size of my palm. It was all in black ink with an intricate filigree pattern making up the entire circle. In the center was something red, but I couldn't make out what it was.

"Shit," the guy swore, snapping my attention away from the design.

Oh, what? Suddenly he was having an attack of conscience now that I was Brody's girl.

Brody's girl. That had a nice ring to it.

Yep. I was definitely delirious.

"We got company!" yelled the guy manning the entrance to the bank. I breathed a sigh of relief. I needed a really big Band-Aid, and I was sure the police had one.

"Send the hostages out," Brody said tersely.

"You crazy?" the man yelled. "The hostages are the only thing keeping them out right now."

"If you send them all fleeing from the building, it will create a few minutes of chaos and will give your team time to slip out the backdoor." Brody reasoned.

Why was he letting them get away?

"You giving us a hand even after I shot your girl?"

"We're brothers. They don't give these tats to anyone."

The man grunted. "Look, man, I'm sorry I shot your girl."

"Shit happens."

Shit. Happens. Really? That's what he had to say about me being shot? Shit happens? If I could've, I would totally kick him. Then stomp on his foot.

"Business has been slow as shit since the busts," the guy went on.

What the hell was this, an interview?

"Yep." Brody agreed, glancing at me, his eyes flocking over my arm and torso.

"I'm going to make it up to you. The bullet in your girl, the suggestion you gave us. We'll cut you in. A couple mil sure will help with the dry spell."

"That's decent," Brody said, offering a fist so they could bang them together.

Men were idiots.

"Everybody out!" ordered the man with the gun. "Run before I change my mind."

There was a momentary lapse of silence when I swear no one breathed. It was like people were trying to decide if they should listen or if it was a trick.

"I said out!" he roared.

People burst into action, racing across the floors. I couldn't see them, but I sure could hear them. Brandy ran by without so much as a glance at me.

I saved her life, yet she was willing to let me lie here and bleed to death. There went her promotion.

I certainly wasn't going die here, so I struggled to sit up, breath wheezing out of my lungs as I struggled into an upright position. I looked down and noted that there was red everywhere. Large dark puddles that saturated my clothes and splattered across the tile like this was some kind of bad horror movie.

The shirt Brody had on my wound started to slip and I reached over to apply pressure and keep it in place. I couldn't stop the whimper that tore out of me.

Brody was there instantly, scooping me up into his arms and cradling me against his bare chest.

As the hostages ran out, screaming and shouting, the men with the duffle bags raced toward the emergency exit at the back. My cheek fell against Brody's chest and he turned to carry me to safety.

"Hey, you coming?" someone yelled behind us.

"I'm taking her to the medics." Brody said.

The sound of a cocking gun drew him up short. He turned. "You got a problem?" he half growled.

"When a man is offered millions of dollars for a job he didn't even plan, he takes it."

"When a man's woman is bleeding, he takes care of her first."

"Bring her." It wasn't really a suggestion.

Brody's entire body stiffened. I saw the flash of horror in his eyes before he banished it away. "What?"

"You know how the crew rolls. We don't leave our members behind. And our women are honorary members."

Brody glanced at me, apology in his eyes.

"Let me put it this way. She comes or she dies," the man growled.

With a tight nod, Brody switched direction and followed after the thieves.

"What the hell are you doing?" I demanded, pain lancing through my body.

"My job," he replied, grim.

What the hell kind of job did this man have?

He leaned in close as we stepped out the back door of the bank. "Trust me, okay?"

I didn't agree or disagree.

It seemed I didn't have a choice.

3

Brody

This wasn't the first time I'd been in a situation like this. In the past, I had robbed stores, been in shootouts, stolen things, dealt drugs, participated in beatdowns, and generally broke the law repeatedly. If I hadn't been under the protection of a badge, I would be rotting in jail.

I was no saint. Hell, I was closer to a sinner than anything.

I couldn't even claim that I was repulsed by some of the stuff I did, because in reality, when you spend two years of your life in the company of thugs, trying to fit in with them, some of their skewed way of life rubs off.

But this was different.

Here I was climbing into the back of some minivan that only a soccer mom would drive while carrying a woman who was shot, bleeding, and needed medical attention.

Being a questionable guy was something I was used to, but dragging in someone who was completely innocent bothered me in ways I didn't care to think about.

I knew the moment their eyes landed on the tattoo. I felt the hush race around the room and their eyes bore into my back, trying to figure out how I got such a mark. I ignored them, focusing instead on Taylor. She was pale, and it worried me.

What the hell did she step in front of that bag for? It was only money. Paper. Worthless when compared to a life.

I never should have halted when I felt that gun between my shoulder blades. I should have disarmed him immediately and taken out as many guys as I could before they got me. I hesitated. I hesitated for several reasons:

1.) I wanted them to think they were in control.

2.) I thought they might punish Taylor for my impulsive actions.

3.) If I jumped into action, they would've wondered who I was.

Hesitation got me in a big fucking mess.

I practically handed them control, they shot Taylor anyway, and they saw the tattoo. They saw the gang symbol that marked me as one of their own, one of the elite crew members who did enough dirty work to earn a permanent mark—a permanent place in the brotherhood on the streets.

It took me two years to earn that tattoo.

It was going to follow me around forever.

And now here I was in the back of a getaway car. At least the hostages got out. I glanced down at Taylor, her face slick with sweat, and the sheen of pain in her eyes made my gut tighten. Rage bubbled up inside me. I wanted to beat every single punk ass in this van. How the fuck did this become my reality?

I was supposed to be driving down the open road. I was supposed to be free of shit like this, at least for a little while.

But no.

Instead, I was dragged right back in and I couldn't walk away. Taylor was tangled up in this mess now and everything I did would come back on her.

I wasn't going to let her be punished for the bad luck that I was at her window when the bank was held up.

I would protect her.

And I would bring these fuckers down.

The symbol on my back gave me an automatic in. The badge attached to my real name gave me the authority to do what I thought was necessary. These guys thought they were getting an ally.

They were wrong.

I glanced out the window, noting we were heading out of downtown Raleigh and traveling into one of the nearby towns. The driver played it smart, not driving erratically, not drawing any kind of attention to the van. He obeyed all the traffic laws and stayed within the speed limit.

A minivan was a good choice because it looked like a mom car, not a criminal mobile. Cops probably wouldn't look twice at it unless it was driving at unusual speeds.

Plus, it had room in the back for all the stolen money.

A million questions bounced around in my head. I wondered where we were going. How long they planned to drive. What their plans were now. But I didn't ask because crew members always played it cool. They always acted like they had things under control. If I started acting fidgety, nervous, or questionable, it would not be good for me. Or Taylor.

I glanced down to find her looking at me. Her green eyes were tight with pain and they latched onto my face as if the only thing anchoring her to consciousness was me.

I felt the weight of her green-eyed stare like an anvil around my neck. I swallowed, trying to get some air past the tight feeling closing my throat. Usually in these situations, the only person I had to look after was myself.

And if I were honest, then I would admit the reason I made such a good undercover cop was because I didn't really care much about what happened to me. They always say the most dangerous man is a man with nothing to lose. Well, that's me. For years I lived by that code. For years I put myself in death's path, pushing the limits, stepping over the boundaries between right and wrong.

It always paid off.

Yet as Taylor's emerald eyes watched me, I felt the chains of responsibility wrap around my chest. Suddenly, I had someone to worry about that wasn't me. Suddenly, the thought of losing the way she held on to me as if her life depended on it seemed like a very big thing.

"Where are we going?" I asked, my voice a little harsher than I intended.

Eyes met mine in the rearview mirror. "You'll see."

"She needs medical attention," I bit out, not caring if I sounded challenging.

Her slim, cold fingers wrapped around my forearm. The impulse to cover her light, cold grip with mine was strong, but my arms were supporting her body and I couldn't risk taking away that support.

"You're gonna be okay," I told her, keeping my voice as low as I could.

Her fingers tightened around my arm.

The van took a sharp turn and I looked up. We were pulling behind an old, abandoned gas station. The parking lot was cracked with weeds growing up between the splits in the pavement. The old pumps were basically silver boxes sticking up out of the ground, long empty. Everything around the building was bare. No houses, no other buildings, no signs of life.

If I hadn't just driven here from downtown Raleigh, I would have thought we were a world away.

The van pulled around the back of the worn-out building and stopped near a boarded-up entrance. With the engine still running, the three passengers started piling out. I sat there for long moments, fighting the urge to demand being taken to a hospital.

One of the guys who said his name was Tommy leaned back inside. "Lucy, we're home!" he said and laughed.

The others in the parking lot laughed and the next thing I knew, they were pulling open the boarded-up door and disappearing inside.

The driver (he said his name was Snake) turned to glance at me. "There's med supplies in there."

The van door slid open with ease and I climbed out, doing my best to not jostle her as I moved. As soon as the van door was shut, the car pulled away, the tail lights glowing red as he retreated. The other three guys were already inside and we were left standing there in the dark, just her and me.

"What's going on, Brody?" she said, her voice hoarse.

"Call me Slater," I reminded her. "It's important you remember that."

"I don't understand what's happening," she said, her eyes flooding with tears.

"I'm going to explain everything real soon." I promised. "First I'm going to patch you up."

"Shouldn't I go to a hospital for that? I have a feeling you aren't a doctor."

I tightened my arms around her. "I'm not a doctor, but I'm a certified EMT. I'll take a look inside and if it's something I can't fix, then I'll blow my cover and get you the hell out of here."

"Your cover?"

I noted the dark coloring of the shirt tied around her arm. The blood had slowed, but not stopped. I needed to stop the bleeding. Explanations were going to have to wait.

"Taylor, listen to me," I intoned seriously, holding her gaze. "This is a bad situation, and I won't lie… It's dangerous as hell. I need you to trust me."

"I don't know you."

"Yeah, and I'm a questionable guy, but I'm not going to let anything happen to you. I'll protect you. It's my job."

"What kind of job do you have?" she said, a hint of exasperation in her tone.

I smirked. "I'm a cop," I whispered against her ear.

Her indrawn breath was confirmation she heard.

She turned her face. My head was still lowered from whispering against her ear and her lips brushed my cheek. I pulled back slightly, aligning our mouths, hovering just inches above hers.

"You with me?" I said low.

She nodded.

Fierce possession took hold of me, sort of like the way a pair of handcuffs felt being slapped around your wrists. I knew how to escape a pair of handcuffs. I wasn't sure I wanted to escape these.

A noise from inside reminded me that this wasn't the time to be feeling things. I straightened and stepped inside the abandoned station.

4

Taylor

I had to be in shock.

There was a reason I wasn't more afraid. There was a reason I wasn't screaming and fighting to get out of Brody's arms and away from this god-awful dirty, abandoned, completely creepy gas station. My body wasn't getting enough blood flow, likely because all the blood was flowing out of me instead of throughout my veins.

It was making me sluggish, slowing my response, and in defense, my body wasn't making adrenaline. So naturally, I felt completely safe in this stranger's arms.

Yeah. That was totally it.

It had nothing to do with the fact that he was shirtless, totally ripped, and covered in tattoos that practically screamed sex appeal. It also had nothing to do with the fact he was wearing a backward baseball cap that screamed thuggish behavior. Thuggish behavior was bad. It was very bad.

But so very good.

The thought caused me to shiver and in reaction to the small movement, Brody pulled me just a little bit closer to his chest. His heat was delicious and I felt my eyes begin to droop. Maybe all I needed was a little nap… just a few minutes to rest my eyes.

"Tay," a nearby voice commanded. "No sleeping."

I grunted in displeasure and forced my eyes back open, looking around the room. If I couldn't sleep, then I would study my surroundings. The place looked the way one would expect an abandoned gas station to look. It was basically a large box with concrete walls and floors that were once covered in linoleum but now were peeling and dirty. In the center of the room were empty racks that likely used to hold merchandise. The counter at the front of the room was bare and crooked, like part of it was sinking into the floor. Behind it on the wall was a sign that read what I assumed was supposed to say QUICK MART except the Q and U were missing so it read as ICK MART.

It was actually very accurate.

The windows were all boarded up, with only slivers of sunlight filtering through, leaving ribbons of light across the dusty and trash-littered floor. Off in the corner was a pile of old brown leaves that would likely lie there until they turned to dust.

On the far end of the room were several large coolers, the kind that sat on the floor and opened from the top. They were no longer working, no longer white, and frankly I would be terrified to go and see what was inside them.

So this is where criminals hung out?

The movies made it look so much more glamorous.

"Down here," one of the men called to Brody, and he pivoted around, following after the men who opened up a hidden door in the wall and disappeared. I could hear their boots clomping down a set of stairs and fear clawed its way up the back of my throat.

I felt my limbs go rigid. They wanted us to go into a basement?

If this is the way the upstairs looked, the basement had to be ten times worse.

"We aren't gonna be here long," Brody reminded me softly.

I peered up at him through the dim lighting. He didn't appear to be bothered at all by this place. If anything, he looked like he'd been in places like this a thousand times before.

Oh, God, I thought. *What if he is lying about being a cop? What if he is really one of these… these criminals, and he's only lying to me so I won't put up a fight?*

The adrenaline was like a shot of ultra-strong espresso being fed right into my bloodstream by an IV. I jackknifed up away from his firm body, flinging out my arm (the one that wasn't shot), and pushing away from him.

He grunted and grasped at me. He was already descending the stairs and my sudden movement caught him off guard. I leapt out of his arms and hit the stair. My legs felt like Jell-O and they buckled trying to support my weight.

I grappled for the railing, only there wasn't one. My nails dug into the side of the wall, dirt and grime pushing its way beneath my fingernails, and my knee bounced off the edge of the crude wooden step.

[35]

"Fucking A," Brody swore, sweeping his arm beneath my armpit and yanking me up before I could go tumbling all the way down.

For long seconds, I dangled in his grasp, renewed pain shooting through my arm, and a sharp ache threatened to crack open my skull.

"So much for trust," Brody muttered, hauling me back into his arms.

Two heads appeared at the bottom of the stairs. "What the hell's going on?"

Brody grunted. "She needs to lose a couple pounds." He groaned as he walked the rest of the way down the stairs.

Yeah, I should have been offended because he just called me fat. But I couldn't summon the energy because my teeth were chattering and my limbs were trembling.

Brody's mouth set in a grim line as he stepped into the basement of horrors. I was aware of him taking in the surroundings like he was a filing cabinet and everything in the room was being filed into a certain folder.

"Where's the med supplies?" he asked.

"Over there," replied the criminal known as Tommy.

I didn't bother to look where he said because lifting my head felt like way too much effort. Brody strode farther into the room and passed through a framed-out doorway that had never been finished.

He lowered me onto a cot, which creaked under my weight as if it too was telling me I was fat.

"Stupid cot," I muttered.

"It's that or the floor," Brody said.

I didn't bother to reply as he moved away out of my immediate line of sight. My heart began to pound, like really threatened to burst right out of my chest. As much as I was leery of him, the thought of him not being here was worse.

I guess that taught me I trusted him more than I thought.

He reappeared and I swallowed, noting the handful of supplies he set on the edge of the cot. He raked over me with assessing eyes, not showing any type of emotion.

"This probably is going to hurt," he said, a muscle in his jaw ticking. "You don't have a choice."

"Just do it," I said. I needed to know how bad this was. I needed to know what I was looking at as far as my injury and being able to get the hell out of here.

Brody pulled away the flannel shirt that was acting as my makeshift blanket. I was already cold and the cool rush of air across my exposed skin only made it worse. My teeth began to chatter a little more loudly, but he acted like he didn't notice.

After setting aside the flannel, it didn't take long to remove the blood-soaked T-shirt that was tied around my arm. I bit my lower lip to keep from crying out. The pain was hot and lancing; it set my entire arm on fire and shot up into my shoulder and down my back. I squeezed my eyes shut and turned my face away from him, toward the wall, as a tear leaked from the corner of one eye and slid down across the bridge of my nose.

"I'm going to clean it," he said softly.

I kept my face turned away as I heard a few little packets being ripped. My body bucked up off the mattress like I was some headstrong bull when the first of whatever he was doing touched the wound.

[37]

I felt his momentary hesitation, and I bit my lip, pinning my body back down and willing him to just get it over with. He seemed to know what he was doing, cleaning away what dried blood he could and then dabbing at the entry wound.

"I'm not going to completely clean it the way it needs," he murmured. "It's already begun to clot on its own and I don't want to disrupt that. Blood loss is a concern and the clotting is the best defense against that."

Yeah, that was good. Clotting was good, a positive sign I might not die. At least not immediately. 'Course, being in a room full of criminals with guns wasn't exactly a good way to keep oneself alive.

"You have burns on your skin," he muttered, his voice turning gravelly. "They shot you at close range. The heat of the bullet burned your flesh."

I felt the coolness of some kind of liquid or ointment, but I didn't turn to see. I didn't want to see. I wanted to maintain what little detachment from this mess I had.

"I'm going to lift your arm," he informed me. "I need to look at the back of it."

I offered my wrist and he took it, lifting my arm up over my head. His fingers probed around and a little sound of discomfort yelped between my lips. Brody stiffened.

"Sorry," I whispered and bit my lip harder as more tears spilled from beneath my lids.

It hurt. It hurt really bad.

He expelled a breath, almost like he was relieved. "It went all the way through the fleshy part of your outer arm."

"If you call me fat one more time I'm gonna scream."

His chuckle was warm and unexpected. It was a momentary distraction from the fire in my arm. "You should be glad you have a little meat on them bones. It protected your arm today."

"So the bullet isn't in there?" I asked, keeping my face turned away.

"No, the exit wound is here," he said quietly as his fingers probed the wound.

I jerked. "Poking at it isn't helping."

"The exit wound is larger than the entry wound, to be expected. The flesh is torn in this area," he said as he applied more of what I assumed was an antiseptic wipe. "Most of the bleeding is coming from here," he said.

He was very matter-of-fact, very clinical, and he seemed to know what he was looking for. Maybe he really was a certified EMT. Maybe I wouldn't die after all.

He tore the wrappers to more stuff, but I didn't dare to look. It wouldn't hurt as much if I didn't see, right?

"I'm going to apply some non-adhesive pads to the entry and exit wounds and then I'm going to wrap your arm in what gauze I have. That should stop the rest of the bleeding and also keep the open wounds protected," he explained as he worked.

His voice was mildly hypnotizing, a very even tone. There wasn't much "up and down" in the sound of his voice. It was steady… like the beat of a heart.

I continued to chew on my lower lip, the motion somewhat distracting me from what else was going on. I couldn't help but wonder what was next. How long would we be here? Would these men just let us go?

My father must be worried sick by now.

He would stop at nothing to find me.

"Sit up," Brody instructed a short while later.

I turned my face and glanced at him. He pushed away from me, picking up the flannel and staring at me expectantly.

I moved slowly, gripping the edge of the cot and trying to lever myself up. My grip was about as strong as a newborn baby's and I couldn't seem to control my own weight. But Brody was there, kneeling alongside the cot, slipping his arm around my waist and physically lifting me into a sitting position. I swung my legs around and a wave of dizziness threatened to knock me over.

"Easy," he whispered. "You lost a lot of blood. You're going to be weak."

After a few moments of steadying myself, I nodded and he moved back, staying at arm's length. He draped the flannel around me, guiding the arm without the bullet hole in through the fabric. When that was finished, I was shaking anew from the effort of holding up my body.

"Keep that arm at your side. Try not to use it or move it. I don't have a sling so you're going to have to pretend there's one there holding your arm in place," he instructed as he pulled the flannel around me gently. His fingers were deft as he buttoned it around my chest.

A scent I identified instantly as his wrapped around my senses. It was deep, exotic, and strong. It seemed to match the person I was becoming to see him as.

He didn't say anything as he reached behind my neck, using his palm to scoop the very long strands of my hair out from under the shirt. He released the mass, running his palm over it, following its length all the way down to the small of my back.

When he reached the end, his palm stuttered, hovering there, creating a pocket of warmth that traveled through my clothes and seeped into my skin. "You're really warm," I whispered, swaying slightly.

"How else are you feeling?" he asked, concern in his tone.

"Like I got hit by a truck."

"Bullets tend to have that effect on people."

"Have you ever been shot?"

He shifted slightly in his crouch, almost like he was settling closer to me. We weren't very far apart and even though I was sitting up, we were almost eye level.

"A couple times." He shifted again, stretching out his torso and pointing to the side of his middle toward a puckered scar. It was round and looked like a knot.

"Is that what mine will look like?" I asked. Without thinking, I reached out and grazed my fingers over the scar. His skin was so warm compared to mine.

"Something like that," he murmured, not moving away from my touch.

Our eyes met and held. Something passed between us, some sort of charged awareness. A feeling of comfort flowed into me. I felt safe with him. This was the scariest situation of my life, yet somehow I knew he would make sure we got out of here.

"I tried to run," I blurted out.

He smiled. "Your ass almost fell down the stairs."

"I'm scared." I admitted, the confession ripping from a deep and private place within me. I might have felt safety in his presence, but I knew we were in danger.

"You should lay down. You look like shit," was his response.

"Way to make a girl feel better," I muttered as I lowered my body against the thin mattress. I tried not to think about all the different kinds of nasty bugs and creatures that were likely living in this thing.

"It's not my job to make you feel better. It's my job to keep you alive."

"You're all about the job, aren't you?" I asked.

He cleared his throat and cut his eyes toward the other men across the room. "You should rest. I'll see if I can find some water."

He moved away from me without a backward glance.

Pain knotted around me, snaring me in its thick and tangled web. I turned back to the dirty cinderblock wall, preferring to stare at it rather than out into the creepy pit of a room.

Maybe after a few moments of rest, I would be able to think more clearly. I could come up with a way to get word to my father.

I could come up with a way to get the hell out of here.

5

Brody

Her wound worried me.

Luckily the bullet passed right through her arm and didn't ricochet off a bone or make its way down into her chest and into an organ. Things could have been much worse for her.

But that didn't mean she was totally out of the woods. I didn't like the way the skin was hot to the touch and red around the edges. It could signal some form of early infection. Or the tissue could just be burned and very damaged from the bullet. Maybe the redness just seemed worse to my naked eye because she still had so much smeared and dried blood on her.

The bottom line was that she needed to be in a sterile environment, the wound needed to be cleaned and stitched, and she needed to be on fluid and antibiotics.

I glanced around the room I followed the three men into. It was practically a cave. All cinderblock walls with sloppily laid grout between. Dust and dirt coated every surface, including the concrete floor. Electrical wires hung out of the exposed ceiling, falling between battered pipes and old duct work.

I brought Taylor into a "private" room just off the main room, if anyone would dare to call it private. There were no walls separating us from the rest of the room, but it seemed someone—a long time ago— attempted to build a wall to close it off because the thick two-by-fours were all erected and nailed into place. But no drywall was ever hung. It's the like the framing was built and then the project was abandoned, the wood left to turn a depressing gray and slowly rot away.

It was musty down here, the air thick with dampness and the scent of mold. Most places in the South didn't have basements, so whatever this place had been likely wasn't good. Hell, it was probably used back then for what it was being used for now: criminal activity.

Besides a small one-person cot (with no blanket or sheet) there was nothing in this "room" other than a single light bulb hanging from a wire in the ceiling. I hadn't tried to turn it on; it probably didn't work anyway.

Out in the main space, there was a ratty mustard-colored couch. It was likely once a nice piece of furniture… oh, about twenty years ago.

It was ripped and dirty and, frankly, just the kind of thing I expected to see in this place. Off to the side was a white mini fridge, a small table with a lamp (which was lit), and a large box, which was serving as a coffee table.

Two of the guys were sitting on the couch, their noses buried in their cell phones, while Tommy was over by the stairs where I figured he was waiting for

Snake. On the other side of the room was a small generator that rumbled in the background. A long black cord ran from the side and I knew that's how they were supplying what little bit of electricity they had.

Over by the wall were quite a few black duffle bags full of stolen money. It was ironic really to see such riches in this rundown, ghetto space.

I glanced at Taylor, making sure her arm wasn't bleeding through the dressing and shirt that covered her. So far I saw no signs of renewed bleeding, but she needed things that this place didn't have.

I shouldn't have brought her here.

I should have just told the crew I was a cop and let them shoot me. At least then Taylor would have gotten the help she needed. And I... well, I wouldn't have to wonder about where to go from here anymore because I'd already be gone.

Thinking like that was a waste of time. The fact was I didn't tell them I was a cop because I wanted them to assume I was an ally. I did nothing but cultivate my identity as Slater Bass for years, even before going completely into their world and cutting off all ties to my old life. So when they started talking to me like I was one of their own, I fell into the role with ease.

I saw it was my opportunity to find out what they were up to, why they were stealing money, what they were doing with it, and what was going on within the organization since me and my buddy Gray brought down a huge drug ring, and along with it, the crew's main operator, Pike.

By the time I realized they would expect me to bring Taylor with me, I was already in. Backing out wouldn't have just gotten me killed, but Taylor as well.

[45]

She was now connected to me, and my actions would follow her.

What I needed to do was win their trust, then get the fuck out of here and take Taylor somewhere safe. If I moved fast, I could have a raid descend on this building before anyone could even think I wasn't coming back.

The money would be returned. More of Pike's crew would be off the streets, and Taylor would be safe.

And I could finally go fishing.

Overhead, the echo of heavy footfalls vibrated the floorboards. Taylor stiffened and glanced at me. I hoped that meant she trusted me enough to keep her safe. Hell, I couldn't blame her if she didn't trust me. Since I showed up, she had gotten shot, kidnapped, and dragged into some dungeon with a bunch of gang members.

Snake walked down the stairs, carrying several more black duffle bags full of cash. He walked over to the pile and tossed them on top, his eyes raking over the massive haul.

He and Tommy fist bumped over their success and then Snake grinned. "Smooth as butter," he bragged.

One of the guys from the couch gave me a cold stare. "Except for the fact we picked up some extra baggage on the way out."

Every crew had a guy like him. A guy with a chip on his shoulder and an ego the size of a small elephant. The only thing a guy like him liked was violence and making everyone else as miserable as he was.

My bet was he didn't even care about the money; he was just in this for the thrill of the kill.

After all, he was the one who shot Taylor.

"You gotta problem with me?" I said, turning full on to face him. I'd take the challenge in his eyes and raise it some. He thought he had a chip on his shoulder? He was the reason Taylor was bleeding. He was the reason I wasn't on the shore fishing right now.

Guys like him were dangerous, but I wasn't exactly Suzie Homemaker.

He pushed up off the couch, dropping his phone on the cushion. "Yeah, maybe I do."

I stepped around the framing toward him. This jackass did not intimidate me. I was pretty pissed off and if he was looking for a fight, I'd sure as hell give him one.

Snake stepped between us and I suppressed an eye roll. I'd wipe the floor with his ass too. "Leo, this ain't the time."

Leo eyed Snake with barely veiled anger. I was waiting for them to start throwing punches at each other. They were young and just pulled off a big heist so I knew their blood was pumping.

To my surprise, Leo backed down. "I don't trust him," he told Snake.

"He helped us get out of the bank," Snake began.

Leo snorted. "It ain't like he shot a bunch of people to clear a path. He made a suggestion. A suggestion any one of us could have made."

"Then why didn't you?" I said, hard.

His eyes narrowed on my face and his hands clenched at his sides.

"Are you saying you don't respect the mark?" Snake challenged, stepping toward Leo. "Are you saying the symbol tattooed on his back isn't a sign he earned his way in, a sign that he already proved his worth to the crew?"

[47]

In any other world, a tattoo might just be a piece of art, a means of personal expression. But here, on the streets, in the gang world... a tattoo was literally life and death. It marked a man clearly on what side he belonged.

"Naw, man." Leo relented. "I know the tat's for real."

"Then what's your problem?"

"The problem is our cut just got smaller."

"But now we got startup fees and another set of hands to get things going." Snake reasoned.

So clearly, Snake was the mastermind of this little group. He was the one in charge.

"Startup fee for what?" I asked, interrupting their little guy time.

Snake swung toward me, eyeing me up like it was the first time he saw me. I didn't squirm under his gaze. In fact, he didn't make me uncomfortable in the least. This guy was small potatoes compared to those I'd worked with before.

"You said you worked for Pike?" he asked, answering my question with one of his own.

"Indirectly. We all worked for Pike, didn't we?"

"So you weren't on his crew in Myrtle?"

"I was for a while. Then I moved to Jacksonville to be part of supply." Basically, I went there to get large shipments of drugs in and take them illegally into Myrtle Beach. But really, that job was just a cover for my real job, solving a murder that the Jacksonville crew leader had committed.

In the end, we brought down that man and he handed over evidence that brought down Pike. All those years of living on the wrong side of the law

[48]

actually counted for something. And it earned me some time off.

Time off which was now being disrupted.

"You were part of the crew that was brought down?" Leo said, a little bit of respect creeping in his tone.

"Yeah, but I wasn't around the night the busts went down." I lied. Actually, I was right in the center of it all, but they didn't need to know that. And all the men who now knew I was undercover were in jail, shipped off to another state. Luckily, the bust went down in Jacksonville and not in Myrtle Beach, so Pike and his inner circle still had no idea who I really was.

Yeah, Pike was in the slammer, but that didn't mean a guy like him didn't have connections on the outside, which is why it was so important for my identity to remain under wraps. The department took a lot of measures to make sure the guys who went down while I was there keep their mouths shut.

And situations like this were exactly why.

"Lucky you," Snake said.

I shrugged.

"So what have you been doing since then?"

I came back to Raleigh. And I did paperwork. Then I did more paperwork. I was debriefed and had my head looked in to make sure being undercover so long hadn't fucked me up too bad.

The thing with being a liar for a living… no one found out anything I didn't want them to know. Even the department shrink. So after the paperwork, the trial, and the mandatory mental health checks, I was cleared to go back to work.

"Laying low. I was on my way out of town today, going fishing." The best lies always have a seed of truth.

I glanced back at Taylor, who hadn't moved from the cot. "I stopped in to see my girl before I left."

"Your girl should know better than to step in front of a man with a gun," Leo said from his position on the couch.

God, I hated him.

I turned from Snake to glare at him. "Maybe you should learn to control your twitchy trigger finger," I said, anger veiled in my words.

"Shoot first; ask questions later," Leo drawled.

"You're an idiot."

He burst up from the sofa, challenge in his posture. I stayed relaxed, like he didn't even bother me. I glanced at Snake. "Hotheads ruin good partnerships."

Snake looked at Leo. "We ain't got time for this."

Tommy walked over to the fridge and pulled out a couple beers. I noted there wasn't any water as he passed some of the alcohol to Leo and his buddy on the couch.

"Now that Pike is gone," Snake began and I looked away from the fridge, "there are some vacancies at the top of the organization."

Organization = gang.

"And you got your eye on the throne," I said.

"I got the ambition, the crew." He gestured toward the duffle bags. "And now I got the capital."

And I had the opportunity to take him down before he even got started.

"I like being on the winning team," I said. "So where do we go from here?"

"Plan is to lay low for a couple days, let the heat die down from the robbery. Then we'll turn some of this money into product and start to expand."

Product = drugs.

Paying cash for a huge shipment of drugs was also a good way to spend the stolen money without raising any red flags, because it would all be done under the radar. And this type of guys wouldn't just walk into a bank with their cut of the profit. These guys would hold their cash and not flaunt it.

I had to admit I was impressed. It was a fairly solid play for one of the top spots in the organization. It was timed right as well. The dust was beginning to settle from the busts, and people within the crew were likely starting to go hungry. Hungry for cash, hungry for work, and likely hungry for someone to call the shots.

Being in the drug business, in an organization like this, was profitable... I should know. I took money from it. That hefty bank account Taylor pointed out wasn't just a product of police force salary alone.

"Solid," I said, letting them know I liked the plan and I was in.

Taylor made a small sound and it put me on alert. This conversation had been damn informative, but it lasted too long.

"Got any water around here?" I asked.

"Got plenty of beer," Tommy offered.

I made a show of grabbing one from the fridge and popping the top. I took a generous swig, casually making my way over to Taylor, when really I wanted to move a lot faster.

Her face was flushed. I knelt down beside her and she stared up at me with pain-heavy eyes. I pressed the back of my hand to her forehead. It was hot.

She was running a fever. Infection was likely taking over her insides like wildfire.

"How ya doing, Tay?"

"Peachy," she replied, her voice low.

[51]

Time to go.

I pushed away and went back into the other room. "I'm going to take her to the hospital, drop her off. We don't need a woman with a bullet wound slowing down our plan."

"We could just take her out right now," Leo offered.

I moved so swiftly no one had time to react. My fist pummeled the side of his jaw, smacking his head to the side as I straddled his body and delivered a few more blows to his face and head.

Snake yanked me off, towing me backward as the other dude on the sofa moved between me and his buddy.

"I swear to God," I growled in his direction, my chest heaving. "You so much as look at her again and I will fucking kill you."

"You're fucking crazy," Leo yelled, dabbing at his bloody lip.

"Chill, man," Snake said, releasing his grip on me. "No one's gonna take out your woman."

Gee, that made me feel a shit ton better.

"I'm taking her outta here," I said, flat.

Snake exchanged glances with Tommy, then looked back at me. "You know you can't take her to the hospital right now. She knows where we are."

"She ain't gonna tell no one."

"She says that now. Then she'll get some feel-good drugs running through her system and her tongue will loosen."

"She needs antibiotics and pain meds," I said.

"So get her some." Snake reasoned.

"You saying I can't take her out of here?"

"I'm saying wait a couple days. On our way to our new location we can drop her off. By that time we'll be on the move and she won't know where we're going next."

"And if I don't like your compromise?" I asked.

The sound of several cocking guns made me glance around the room. All four men had drawn on me.

Snake gave me an apologetic look. "It's just business, man. You understand."

Oh, I understood I was going to nail his ass to the wall for this. "If we're gonna be here a couple days, I gotta go get some supplies."

Snake smiled. "Van's parked about half a mile away." He tossed me the keys. I caught them in midair.

I started toward Taylor, sorry I was going to have to move her but seeing no other choice.

"Leave her," Snake's voice stopped me in my tracks.

I turned back. "What?"

"I said leave her," he said. "Think of it as a proof of trust," he explained when I only stared at him. "We'll know we can trust you to come back without pulling a fast one and you'll know you can trust us when you see we've kept your girl safe."

He wanted me to leave her. Here. Alone.

She needed those meds. Without them she might die.

If I didn't agree to this "proof of trust," they'd probably kill us both right now.

I gave a swift nod and all the guns disappeared. Tommy and Snake went back to drinking beer and Leo and his buddy, whose name still remained a mystery, went back to their phones. I leaned over Taylor, speaking so hopefully only she could hear.

"I'm going to go get you something to make you feel better."

Her eyes widened and she reached for my arm. "Don't leave me here."

"I got to, Taylor. They won't hurt you while I'm gone." That was probably the worst lie I'd ever told.

"I have a bullet hole in my arm from one of them."

"Which is exactly why I gotta go out."

She looked at me intently for long moments. Her feverish eyes grew moist with tears. "You're going to come back, aren't you?"

"I swear on all that's holy on this planet I'm coming back." I cupped her cheek in my palm. "I promise."

She nodded, her hand sliding off my arm. It seemed like something someone who was entirely defeated would do.

"Hey," I said, stroking her cheek with my thumb. Her green eyes looked up once more. "Don't give up."

"I won't."

I smirked. "Do me a favor, huh? Don't try to run while I'm gone. Those assholes will let you fall down the stairs."

Her lips cracked into a small smile. It felt like a major victory.

"Bring me a Gatorade."

I smiled.

"And a really big Tylenol."

My chest swelled a little with her spoken words. Most women would be screaming and crying. Hell, most men would be whimpering like babies. I knew she was scared. She was wounded and confused. Yet she was keeping it together.

I liked her. She was tough.

[54]

"I'll see ya soon."

She nodded.

I pulled away. Walking out of that ghetto, rundown building was one of the hardest things I'd ever done. But I didn't have a choice. As soon as I cleared the empty parking lot, I upped my pace into a run.

I had antibiotics and Gatorade to find.

And I also had a phone call to make.

6

Taylor

Time slowed to a crawl.

I felt every single second, every single breath I drew, and every single lump on this craptastic cot.

I even counted the cracks in the wall. I lost interest at twenty.

Chills racked my body and it hurt to shake. Every little jolt my body forced upon itself sent ripples of pain scattering across my body.

Where was he? How long had he been gone?

Lying here and waiting for a man to come back and save the day wasn't really my idea of a good time. In fact, it made my already foul and emotional state worse.

I attempted to blink away the dizziness in my eyes and swallow back the dryness of my throat. Maybe I could get ahold of a gun. It would likely be the only way I'd get out of here without being tackled to the ground.

I definitely wasn't a helpless damsel in distress, but being injured and sick took away a lot of my strength and power.

As I was lying there hatching ideas for the best way to get a gun, a cell phone rang. *Oohh, I could get ahold of a cell phone!* I thought excitedly.

I could pretend I was passing out or something, turn into one of those whiny, demanding females, and get one of them over here. Maybe they would drop their cell phone and I could use it to dial 9-1-1.

I sure as hell hoped I didn't get the same operator as before.

She had been sooo not helpful.

"Yeah," Snake said, interrupting my very brilliant planning. I glanced his way, watching him hold the phone up to his ear. A second passed while he listened. "So what did you find out about Slater?"

My ears perked up at the mention of Brody (aka Slater) and my stomach knotted with nerves. What if he found out Brody was really a cop? They would kill him when he came back... and worse...

They would kill me.

I was a hopeful person. I always had faith that my death would come when I was in my nineties, after I lived a full life, and I would pass quietly in my sleep in my own bed. I never imagined I might die by the hand of a gang member at the age of twenty-four.

"Yeah," Snake said, listening. "That long?" he muttered.

Oh, how I wished I could hear what was being said on the other end of the line.

"Okay, tight," he said into the line. "Uh-huh." As he talked, he paced around the room and I watched his movements carefully, trying to read his body language.

So far he didn't seem like someone told him there was a cop involved. He didn't seem like anything he was learning was going to result in a gunfight.

[57]

That was good.

Just as my nerves started to settle, Snake came to a halt. "You don't say?" he muttered and then pivoted around.

I didn't bother to look away, to hide the fact I was looking at him.

Our eyes met.

"Yo, thanks for the info, man. You hear anything else, dial me." He spoke into the phone, but his eyes were still on me.

I didn't like the way he was looking over here. I was hoping he'd forget about me.

He pulled the phone away from his ear, slipping it into the pocket of the black pants he wore. True to his name, he practically slithered across the floor toward me. The look in his eyes was calculating and a little mean.

I felt my fingers curl into my palm, gripping at the fabric covering my legs.

Oh my God, he knew about Brody.

He knew he was a cop and now he was going to kill me.

7

Brody

I needed a shirt. Walking around without one would just draw unwanted attention. Not to mention, I wanted to keep the gang symbol on my back covered.

The air was still hot as hell even though the sun was lowering in the sky. Raleigh had two temperatures throughout the year: hot and Hades. The van was right where Snake said it would be, and I jumped in, turning the AC on high and pointing it toward the closet town, Garner.

I thought about driving back into Raleigh to get my cell phone and weapon out of my truck, but it had likely been impounded because it was sitting outside the bank at the time of the robbery and I was nowhere to be found.

I knew the guys at work would know I was likely already working the case, but not everyone on the PD would know, so if I was spotted in Raleigh, I might get hauled in for questioning and that would not help Taylor at all.

Leaving her back there was pretty dangerous and I didn't want to be gone any longer than absolutely necessary. About two minutes of driving brought me into Garner. Just like that, I was in a quaint town of North Carolina.

I slowed and turned into the nearest gas station and parked alongside the building. I bypassed the "No Shirt, No Shoes, No Service" sign stuck to the glass double doors and stepped inside.

There was a girl with a high ponytail behind the counter, looking bored, but as soon as she saw me, she perked up, standing up straight and giving me a onceover. I gave her a smile and wandered over to a rack of T-shirts that were hanging nearby.

They were all white, sporting red NC State University logos, with the words Wolf Pack written directly beneath. I selected an extra-large off a hanger and held it up. "You mind?"

I asked the girl. She blushed.

I pulled the shirt over my torso and then reached for the last remaining hoodie on the rack. It was a large, but at least it would be warm. I took the shirt and went toward the back where I stood in front of the selection of Gatorade, pondering what flavor Taylor might like.

Wait.

Was I seriously standing here debating over the flavor of Gatorade for some chick?

I didn't have time for that shit.

So I reached in and pulled out about five, loading up my arms and then going into the snack isle. There wasn't exactly a healthy selection, but I'd take what I could get. I piled some junk and some over-the-counter pain meds on top of the drinks and traipsed to the counter and dropped it all in front of the girl.

"Don't forget the shirt I'm wearing," I told her as she rang up everything.

She giggled and I handed over a few twenties. Once everything was in a bag, I headed down the road, not stopping until I saw the next place on my list. I parked near a side entrance, hoping I would get lucky and it wasn't one of those doors that was an emergency exit only with one of those annoying alarms.

I bypassed it and went in the front entrance, walking right up to the counter in the center of the room. The receptionist barely looked up when I signed the log on the counter, using some made-up name.

"You need to be seen today?" she asked.

Why the hell else would I walk into an Urgent Care clinic in the middle of the day? "Yeah," I said, keeping my voice low. "Think I might have strep." I lied.

"Sign in," she said, obviously not seeing me already doing so. "We'll be with you shortly."

I guess I wasn't the only one lying today. She and I both knew that "shortly" meant four hours.

"Can I use the restroom?" I asked.

She pointed off to her right. "Through that door."

Bingo. It was on the other side of the waiting room, behind the door where they called the patients back. "Thanks," I said and headed straight toward the bathroom. On my way in, I noted the nurse's station just two doors down from the bathroom. And across from that was the exit that I parked near.

It didn't appear to have an alarm attached to it.

I stepped in the bathroom and took a piss. Then I washed my hands and listened against the door for any kind of movement in the hall outside. I could hear someone talking nearby and then their voice retreated and I heard a door close down the hall.

The bathroom door opened soundlessly, and I peered out, not seeing anyone nearby. Stepping out into the hall, I kept my footfalls soft as I moved stealthily across the hall into the nurse's station. I had maybe one minute tops to get what I needed and get the hell out. The first place I went was to the white overhead cabinets hanging above a cheap countertop. Inside, I found packaged sterile syringes and various sizes of bandages. I grabbed several of everything I thought I might need and then turned to the cabinet behind me. I found several vials of amoxicillin and carefully stuffed them into my pockets. Footsteps down the hall had me grabbing handfuls of other supplies and shoving them into my hat.

A few seconds later, I was peaking into the hall, and once it was clear, I held my breath as I pushed through the side door.

My muscles were tense and ready as I waited for the piercing sound of an alarm to draw attention my way. Even if it went off, I wasn't giving up these supplies. They wouldn't be able to catch me before I drove away.

Thankfully, no alarm sounded, and I let out a breath. A nurse turned the corner just as the door shut and I took off for the van. I waited until I was out of the parking lot and down the street before I carefully pulled everything out of my pockets and hat and placed it into the bag with the hoodie.

The clock on the dashboard showed I'd been gone thirty minutes already. Thirty minutes that felt like a damn lifetime. Now that I had what I needed to help make Taylor comfortable, I wanted to put the pedal to the metal and get back there, but I still had one more stop to make.

There was a Dunkin Donuts down the street so I parked in the lot and went inside, getting in line. There was a kid who looked to be about college age running the register, and he looked like he really loved his job (not). When it was my turn, I walked up to the counter and ordered two dozen donuts, several coffees, and a large latte with caramel in it.

I handed over cash for the order and then dropped a ten-dollar bill in the tip jar right in front of the kid.

"Thanks," he said, his eyes lighting up at the cash.

"You happen to have a pay phone in here?" I asked while I waited for him to fill up two flat boxes with the donuts. "My cell phone died, and if I don't call my girlfriend and tell her when I'll be home, she'll give me a two-hour lecture when I get there."

The guy snorted. "Women." Then, he said, "Nah, we don't have a payphone. Do they even make those anymore?"

God, how old was this kid? He'd probably never even seen a payphone before.

"Lecture it is," I said ruefully.

The kid glanced around. "Here, you can use my cell real quick. Take it over there so my supervisor doesn't see. I'm not supposed to have it in my pocket."

"Sweet," I said, taking it as he slid it across the counter.

He went off to make the coffees, and I stepped over to the corner of the restaurant, dialing Mac's private cell phone.

Mac was the chief at the PD and I knew he was probably waiting for my call.

"Who the hell is this?" he demanded when he answered.

"It's West," I replied, keeping my voice muted.

[63]

"What the hell have you gotten yourself into now, West?" he growled into the phone.

"Just a normal day at the office," I replied, leaning against the large window and scanning the room for anyone overly interested in my conversation.

The place wasn't very busy. It was late afternoon and most people already got their caffeine fix for the day.

"Where are you?" he asked, his tone turning serious.

"The snake we chopped the head off of is growing a new head."

He was silent a moment. I knew he would understand what I was telling him. "That's what the heist was about? Startup funds?"

"Yes."

"Did they force you and the girl out with them?"

"I went willingly,"

"Why the hell would you do that, West?" he demanded.

"Did you take your blood pressure pill today?" I asked.

He made a choking sound.

As much as I enjoyed ribbing him, I didn't have time right now. "They saw the mark. They brought me into the fold. They assume the girl is with me. She needs medical attention." I turned and lowered my voice. "About two miles outside of Garner there is an old abandoned gas station. You'll find what you're looking for beneath it."

"Can you hold out a few more hours, until we get a team in place and we have the cover of night?"

"Yeah. Make sure you have an ambulance on standby."

"Are you hit, West?" he asked, concerned.

"No. She is."

Mac swore. "Keep her alive, West. She—"

I cut him off. The kid behind the counter was setting my complete order on the counter and glancing my way.

"I will. See you in a few." I disconnected the line and then quickly erased the call from the phone's history.

I lifted my chin to the kid behind the counter and slid it across to him as I lifted the two boxes of donuts. I balanced them with one arm and reached for the beverage holder full of coffee.

"Thanks, man," I told him.

"Have a good one," he said.

I highly doubted the rest of my day was going to be very good. But at least by tonight, all this shit would be over. With my testimony, the presence of the stolen money, and Taylor's bullet wound, the case against these clump nuggets would be airtight.

Taylor would go to the hospital, and I could go fishing.

I wasn't sure why, but suddenly, fishing wasn't as appealing as it seemed this morning.

8

Taylor

I forced myself up into a sitting position, the long-lost adrenaline finally finding its way into my system.

If this guy wanted to kill me, I wasn't going to make it easy for him.

I glanced around for a weapon, but of course there wasn't one. I eyed the two-by-fours nailed between the spaces and wondered if they were fragile enough to dislodge one so I could wield it.

My stomach roiled, the meager contents of the latte and croissant I ate this morning threatening to make a reappearance. I leaned back against the wall, using it as a support for my broken body. Using my uninjured arm, I tried to pull the flannel around me a little more, needing more warmth and unable to find it.

I knew I was running a fever. The way my body ached and shook was proof. I also knew a fever wasn't a good sign. I wondered how much longer I could sit down here without treatment before I became too sick to function.

"Seems your boy Slater has quite the reputation," Snake said, stopping in front of the cot to stare down at me.

I didn't bother to answer because I wasn't sure what kind of reputation he was referring to. I prayed it wasn't the reputation of a cop.

He smirked. "You didn't know, did you?"

"Know what?" I asked, my voice weak.

"Slater is quite a ladies' man. A player. You know you're probably not the only girl he keeps around."

So *that's* what this was about? Brody was a player? This wasn't about his real identity coming to light. This wasn't about me being killed as a message to the nark. This was about mental abuse. Snake thought he would have some fun at the expense of the bleeding girl on the cot.

"I never asked him for a commitment," I said, lifting my chin.

He grinned. "He wouldn't give you one anyway. I heard all about how he has a lady in every crew, a girl in every bar. In fact, he only did the bare minimum of work in Jacksonville because he was too busy burying his face in some girl's cleavage."

What a lovely picture that painted. My stomach soured just a little bit more.

"What's your point?" I spat.

Snake leaned down in from of me, his body brushing up against my knees. He was a tall guy, a little on the thin side, with a buzzed head, dark eyes, and eyebrows that seriously needed a wax. His nose was crooked like it had been broken and his teeth were yellowed likely from smoking the cigarettes of which he reeked.

He had a greasy look about him and I really wasn't surprised. He probably was around my age, and he was definitely not my type.

He pulled a gun out of the waistband of the back of his pants and laid it beside me on the cot, the muzzle pointing at my thigh.

You know, it pissed me off. I wasn't in the mood to look at guns. I wasn't in the mood to get shot again.

"What the hell do you want?" I breathed.

He reached out and touched a strand of hair. "I've always had a thing for gingers." he replied, smiling.

I forced back a gag.

"Since you don't seem to mind sharing Slater, maybe he wouldn't mind sharing you."

"I'd mind," I said, looking him straight in the eye.

"Why roll with a beta when you could belong to an alpha?" he said.

Was I supposed to swoon? That wasn't going to happen. Ever.

"I don't belong to anyone but myself."

He reached around the back of my neck and yanked me forward. I felt some of the gauze wrapped around my arm yank free and a gush of warmth under my arm.

"I like a woman that knows how to use her mouth."

Really? I swear this loser could write a book on the worst pickup lines in history.

He brought his face closer and I readied my teeth. I'd bite him if he came any closer. Yeah, it would get me shot again, but I'd rather take another bullet than let his smarmy mouth touch me.

The heavy sound of footfalls overhead sent relief collapsing over me. Brody was back. Snake looked up at the ceiling and then back at me, giving me a smirk. The door to the basement opened with a creak, and I saw Brody's jean-clad legs come into view.

Snake was looking in his direction so I took advantage of his stupidity and grabbed up the gun, pointing it right at his temple. He swallowed, his Adam's apple bobbing in his throat.

"Get your hands off me," I said low, enjoying the heavy weight of the metal in my palm.

Snake removed his hand from the back of my neck and backed up a little. Brody stopped in the center of the room, watching the situation unfold.

The other guys in the room all pulled out their guns, aiming them in my direction. Still, I didn't lower mine. I didn't feel good, I was thirsty, and I was pissed.

"What the hell is going on?" Brody asked.

"Your woman is whacked," Snake said, backing away from me.

"I like my bitches crazy," Brody said. I considered turning the gun on him.

Before I could make up my mind, he crossed the room, stepped in the path of the gun, and wrapped his hand around the barrel. His eyes met mine. I saw the concern shading the espresso color and the toughness inside me seemed to fizzle out.

He took the gun and tucked it in the waistband of his jeans.

"That's my gun," Snake said, stepping forward.

"I know you got more than one," Brody reasoned.

Shit. I hadn't even thought of that.

Snake shrugged.

"I brought some donuts and coffee," he gestured, and for the first time since he walked in I smelled the sweet pastry and the warm rich scent of coffee.

"That's decent of ya," Tommy said, already shoving a glazed donut into his mouth.

Brody didn't even glance at me when he walked across the room, picked up a Styrofoam cup, a couple bags, and came back. He set everything on the edge of the cot and extended the cup to me.

"Drink this," he said. "It's warm."

My stomach revolted at the thought of putting anything in it, but my fingers practically shouted *Amen!* when the heat seeped into my stiff joints.

Brody glanced back at the others, who were all involved in the food and coffee he brought, laughing over something on someone's phone. He glanced back at me. "Did he hurt you?"

I shook my head, taking in the presence of his shirt and the way it stretched across his shoulders.

"Thanks for getting me a gun."

"I didn't get it for you. I got it for me." I gave him a look, hoping he would get the point and hand it over.

He grinned. "I'm a better shot than you."

"How do you know?" I asked, lifting an eyebrow.

"'Cause you're a girl."

"You did not just play the 'I'm the man' card, did you?"

He grinned again. He had one of those naughty grins that probably charmed the panties off all those women Snake said he had.

That thought made me a lot less charmed.

Brody gave me a curious glance. "What is it?" He frowned. "Are you feeling worse?" He laid the back of his hand against my forehead and glanced at my arm.

"Please tell me you got some Tylenol."

With one hand, he dumped out the contents of the bag on the end of the cot. I turned my head to look at it all, but another wave of dizziness had me pressing more firmly against the wall.

"Drink that," he ordered, sifting through the items.

My hand shook as I lifted the heavy cup to my lips and tilted it so the warm liquid spilled onto my tongue. It was a latte and it was really sweet... It tasted like caramel and whipped cream.

I swallowed the sweet concoction, which made a path all the way down into my stomach. It was good so I took another sip.

Using his teeth, he ripped open a pack of what looked like Advil and dumped several pills into his palm. "I wasn't sure what kind of Gatorade you like." The look on his face was sheepish.

I looked down to see five bottles of the stuff lying across the cot. A small smile curved my lips. "You got one of every color?"

How sweet was he?

"Which one do you want?" he asked, gruff, like he was embarrassed he'd done something so sweet.

"Purple."

"Figures," he muttered and grabbed it up, uncapped the lid, and then traded me the latte. "Open," he ordered, holding the pills against my mouth. I told myself the sudden chill was just another side effect of the fever and not because his fingers brushed my lips.

I did as he asked and he dropped the pills on my tongue. I swallowed them down with a few great gulps of the drink. I felt the cool liquid slosh around in my belly and it made me squirm uncomfortably. I willed myself not to throw up. I needed those meds and I had to keep them down.

I dropped the Gatorade in my lap and he moved it. Before handing the coffee back to me, he raised it to his lips and I watched his throat work as he swallowed.

One of his tattoos stretched up a little above the neckline of his T-shirt, and I stared at the way it practically caressed the side of his throat. Brody lowered the drink, catching my stare, and we sat there for long moments, studying one another... like we weren't in a serious situation, like this was some casual meeting.

"Here," he said finally, his voice for my ears only, surrendering the cup to my cold hands.

He reached for the buttons on my shirt and I froze. "What the hell are you doing?"

"What do you mean?" he asked, rocking back on his heels. "I thought that moment we just had counted as foreplay... That wasn't an invitation to second base?"

I snorted. "You would think that."

His eyes narrowed and a little chill raced up my spine. How he went from playful to intimidating in a matter of seconds was unsettling. "What the hell does that mean?"

I motioned with my chin toward Snake and his fellow thugs. "He had you checked out," I whispered.

Brody grunted, not seeming surprised at all. He began to rifle through the stuff on the bed, lining up what looked like legit medical supplies. "Where did you get all that?"

"I stole it."

"You stole medicine for me?" I asked, oddly touched by his criminal activity.

The next thing I knew I was going to be a guest on the Dr. Phil show titled: "When Bad Boys Happen to Good Girls."

"You needed it." He shrugged. Then he reached for the buttons again. This time I didn't stop him as he began to unfasten the flannel around me.

"What did he find out?" Brody asked low as he leaned forward to peel the shirt away from my body.

"Apparently you have quite a reputation with the ladies."

His teeth flashed white when he pulled back. "When a guy spends eighty percent of his time making out with a girl in a corner, no one ever thinks he's listening to their conversation."

Eighty percent of his time? "Holy crap, that's a lot of girls."

He sat back, abandoning his first aid efforts. "I find it interesting that I just told you my secret to recon and all you heard was the amount of time I spent making out."

I blushed.

He smiled and leaned close. "Be a good girl and let me fix you up, and then maybe I'll give you one of my famous kisses."

"Your kisses are famous?" I whispered, silently cursing my sudden one-track mind. Damn if my lower belly wasn't tightening with the thought of his lips caressing mine.

He didn't seem fazed at all about the thought of kissing me. Meanwhile, I was sitting here melting into a little puddle, trying not to drool.

Get ahold of yourself, Taylor! I demanded and averted my attention to the many vials of liquid next to me. And beside those were needles.

[73]

Cambria Hebert

"What the hell is all that?" I asked.

"Antibiotics, a local numbing agent," he said, searching through it all. "And real bandages."

"You're not sticking me with a needle." I refused, shaking my head and shrinking against the wall. "Just give me another pill."

He seemed amused. "You need the antibiotics."

"How about just a Band-Aid?"

He nodded and I sighed. "You can have one of those too. After you get a shot."

I scowled and held the coffee between us like a shield. "Stay where you are," I ordered.

Gently, he took the cup from my grasp and pulled it away, sitting it off to the side on the floor. "Are you afraid of a little needle, Taylor?" he murmured.

"Maybe." I hedged.

He picked up some kind of wipe and ripped it open, cleaning his hands. Then he reached for another white, wrapped item labeled STERILE SYRINGE and ripped it open.

I shook my head as my knees began to shake. "Get that thing away from me."

He ignored me and picked up one of the vials and inserted the very pointy needle into the top, slowly drawing some of the liquid into the body of the syringe. "And here I was thinking what a tough girl you were for taking a bullet and barely even complaining."

"Needles hurt," I squeaked.

He smiled a smile that made the corners of his eyes crinkle. "They don't hurt that bad."

I disagreed.

Holding the injection in one hand, he opened another wipe and swiped down the side of my good arm.

[74]

"You are not giving me a shot."

"You're a terrible patient," he scolded, setting aside the wipe and leaning close to me. I never noticed how full his lips were until he pursed them, blowing out a stream of oxygen over the damp area the wipe left behind. The breath in my own throat caught. The sensation of his breath moving over my skin heightened my senses. In that moment, I felt hyper aware of him.

"I am not," I argued, but it was a halfhearted attempt.

"Your breath smells like coffee," he whispered, dropping his chocolate gaze to my lips.

Just his stare made them tingle. Automatically, I pressed them together, trying to make the sensation stop (or maybe cause it to last longer).

"Have you ever been kissed so good that everything else in the room falls away?" he murmured, brushing the soft pad of his thumb along the edge of my lower lip. "Has a man ever wrapped himself around you so completely that you forgot to think?"

I swallowed, my head swimming at the picture he was painting. The truth was no kiss had ever affected me like that. It was probably why I was still single. Well, that and my father ran off every guy who showed interest in me. He was an unapproachable man, and most men were easily intimidated.

"Tay," he said, once again calling me by the shortened version of my name. Usually when someone tried to call me that, I bit their head off. But when Brody said it, my insides felt like a snowman on a too-hot day… dissolving into a damp puddle.

"Hmm?" I replied.

"Have you?"

I shook my head.

His lips hovered just over mine while his free hand teased my skin by drawing little circles over the inside of my elbow, and every breath he pulled in pushed his body just a little bit closer to mine. "Would you like to?"

I was drunk just from the sound of his voice. I was hung over from the heat radiating from his body, and I was totally lulled by the gentleness of his touch.

I nodded, a very slight movement of my head. There was no point in lying; my body, my eyes, and even my trembling limbs would betray me.

He dipped just an inch closer, his lips skimming, barely grazing mine, and I sighed at the contact, waiting for him to deepen the kiss.

But he didn't.

He pulled back swiftly, pinched my arm, and stuck me with the needle.

I yelped as he depressed the end, flooding my system with antibiotics. But the thing was it didn't hurt, not at all. I was still too tangled up in the fact he hadn't kissed me. He hadn't done to me what he said he would.

And for that I was sorely angry.

Angry at myself for falling for it but also at him for not following through.

"You're an ass," I said when he pulled away the needle and covered the puncture with a small square of gauze.

"I don't deny it." He agreed, dropping the needle beside us and swooping in, taking me off guard yet again.

This time his lips didn't graze mine. They didn't taunt my senses. His mouth latched onto mine as if he were a seed and my lips were enriched soil, giving him a place to settle, a place to bloom and grow.

Sadly, I didn't have much experience in the kissing department, but even so, I didn't have time to be nervous or self-conscious. It was like his mouth knew exactly where to go, exactly how to move against mine to draw out exactly the response he wanted.

And the response was nothing short of devastating.

He might have been the one in control, yet I felt like everything he did was entirely about me.

The inside of his lip was silky smooth, slightly moist from the heat of his mouth, and every time his lips brushed against mine, I could feel that part of him. It was almost like that feeling you got when you jumped into a pool and water glided across your bare skin for the first time.

Gentle pressure built inside me as we kissed. Brody sucked my lower lip into his mouth, gently tugging on it, teasing its fullness with his tongue. It felt so incredibly right that my hand wrapped around his neck and pulled him closer, demanding more.

The bill of his hat bumped against the back of my hand and I knocked it away, sending it falling to the floor. Ignoring the protest in my arm, I grasped his jaw and pushed my hands around the back of his head, moving upward, raking my palms over the buzzed cut he wore. His hair was thick and it tickled my hands as I moved.

Brody's hand traveled across my waist, where his fingers dug into the flesh just above my hipbone. The pleasure of his hand and mouth on me simultaneously created a sensation close to desperation, like I was a clock that was wound entirely too tight.

Just when I thought I couldn't take any more, he pulled away his hand and lifted his lips, angling his head so he was kissing me from a brand new direction.

His tongue stroked against my lips, almost requesting permission to come closer, and I opened immediately, wanting to feel the texture of his tongue, wanting part of him inside me.

He broke the kiss, rocking back on his haunches. I blinked, gazing at him with a bemused feeling clouding my head. I watched in apt fascination as he swiped his thumb along his lower lip and then stuck it in his mouth, almost like he was sucking off what was left of me on his lips.

"I like the way you taste," he told me, his gaze dropping back to my lips.

Damn.

I was shot, kidnapped (technically), in danger, dirty, cold, and sitting in a grungy gangster hideout… yet true to his word, he made me forget it. In that kiss, I found more than passion; I also found escape. He was like balm to my open wounds, a blanket to my shivering insides, and an umbrella to the storm raging above my head.

And he liked the way I tasted.

"You taste pretty good too," I finally said, speech finding its way back into my brain.

He smirked and reached for a Band-Aid, ripping off the little tabs and then smoothing it over the spot where he gave me the shot. "It didn't hurt, did it?" he asked, his voice smug.

"I still don't like needles."

"That's too bad because I'm not done yet."

Part of me hoped I'd get a kiss like that for every needle he picked up.

9

Brody

Taylor was definitely no shrinking violet. But her bravery bordered on stupidity.

Finding her holding a gun on Snake was pretty amusing. What wasn't amusing was the fact she didn't seem to realize brandishing a gun did not give her that much control. She was weak, outnumbered, and obviously didn't realize these guys were professionals at this.

Clearly, this girl couldn't be left alone because, clearly, she was a hazard to herself and her own safety.

And then she went and chose a purple Gatorade. Purple. The damn girliest color known to man.

If that wasn't bad enough, as she was sipping that lavender-colored concoction, she goes and looks at the needles like they're alien babies come to take over her body.

Not many people surprise me.

But she did.

Her entire being was one big conundrum, a contradiction in heels.

On one hand, she portrayed a sort of tomboy personality (despite being flawlessly beautiful), showing a set of balls most women didn't possess. Giving tips on fishing, standing up for people in bad situations, taking a bullet like a champ, and then pulling a gun on a known gangster.

I thought I had her figured out. I thought I knew what to expect from her.

Then she went and picked that damn purple Gatorade and became shaky as a newborn filly when presented with a needle.

It was almost as if beneath her tough exterior was a girly girl with the bite of a mouse.

I really hadn't meant to kiss her. I only meant to distract her from the fact I was about to stick a needle in her arm. The distraction worked… but her honest reaction left me unable to leave it at only a distraction.

Her breathing stalled; her body stilled. I literally felt the anticipation rolling off her. It made me wonder how in the hell no one had managed to claim her yet, how she could say that no one ever kissed her so good that she forgot where she was.

I wasn't about to back away from that challenge. Yet the second I closed the distance between us, it became more than proving a point. It became about giving her something I knew no one else had. It became about filling my mouth with nothing but the taste of her.

She sent my senses into overdrive and my cock to twitching in my jeans. I wanted to jam my tongue so badly inside her mouth. I wanted to explore the very depths of her until I too was completely lost.

But this wasn't the time or place.

I couldn't afford to be distracted like this.

[80]

And she couldn't afford to keep bleeding.

It didn't help that when I broke our lips apart, she looked sorely dazed and disappointed. Her lips were swollen and round, glistening from the faint moisture in our kiss.

"I have a local numbing agent here. It will numb up the area where you're wounded and take away a lot of the sting. Once it takes effect, I'm going to clean you up and bandage you better."

She made a face like I tried to feed her something very distasteful. It made me smile.

"Here," I said, pushing the coffee cup back into her hand. "Drink some more of this."

She took it and sipped dutifully while I opened some of the bandages and wipes. We didn't speak as I unwrapped the crude bandaging I applied to her arm earlier. I wasn't surprised when I noted the non-adhesive pads were soaked with blood. The one on the back of her arm, where the bullet exited her body, was worse.

She watched me with a stony expression when I filled yet another syringe with numbing agent.

"This isn't going to feel good," I warned her, leaning close to find a place to inject her.

Taylor turned away her face, gazing toward the back wall as her fingers twisted themselves in the front of my T-shirt.

The action endeared her to me even more. Once again, she was making me feel like I was her anchor, her lifeline through this mess. I never wanted to be responsible for someone else... but right now it didn't seem like it would be that bothersome.

"Ready?" I whispered.

She squeezed her eyes closed and I pierced her skin.

I heard her breath catch and her fingers tightened on my shirt. I worked as quickly as I could, injecting the medicine and trying to move it around the area.

"It shouldn't take long to work," I said, pulling back. She didn't say anything so I used one of the empty bags and picked up all the trash and wrappers I'd already used. Taylor didn't look at me or her arm. She kept her face turned away and her fingers twisted in my shirt.

"Tell me if you can feel this," I whispered and dragged two fingers over the inside of her wrist. She shivered. I stroked her again, this time applying a bit more pressure. "Can you feel that?"

"Mmm-hmm," she confirmed, sounding like a purring cat.

Unable to help myself, I trailed my fingers upward, across the inside of her arm and up her bicep. When I got to the wounded area, I began poking at the red and swollen flesh. I used harder jabs than before, but I really wanted to be sure she was numb.

"I can't feel that," she said, relieved.

"That's good. I'm going to clean it up and then stitch the worst of it closed."

Her head snapped up. "You're going to stitch it?"

"Best way to keep the blood inside you where it belongs." I felt the side of my lip curling up.

"Fine." She sighed.

The lighting in here sucked so I scooted as close as I could and got to work. Because she was numb, I was able to work faster and do a better job of cleaning her up this time around.

After putting several stitches in the front and back of her arm, I decided to cover the wound, just for added protection because we were in such a dirty pit. I layered the large square pads I swiped from the office and used medical tape to secure them in place.

When I was just about finished, she turned her head. We were so close to each other I could make out the lighter flecks of green in her eyes.

"Are we going to get out of here?" she whispered, her eyes seeking the truth in mine.

"I swear it." I vowed, something knotting in the center of my chest.

I knew she wanted to ask me how I knew, how exactly I could be so certain. But I couldn't risk telling her about my phone call, about the raid that was being planned right this moment.

"Trust me," I whispered.

"I do." Taylor moved to turn her head away, but I grasped her chin and brought her back.

"Why?" I demanded. I had to know the reason she went from trying to run away from me to believing I wouldn't let her down.

"Because you came back," she whispered.

I released her chin and stroked the side of her cheek, noting the way her faint freckles stood out over her alabaster skin. I couldn't imagine anyone leaving her behind.

"Drink some more of that," I said, gruff. "You're pale and cold."

I turned back to the bandages, trying to understand why my heart was beating so erratically as I finished up and pulled the flannel shirt away from her. She gasped and tried to pull it back.

[83]

"I got you something warmer," I said, reaching beneath me and pulling out the large NC State hoodie. I held it up for her to see.

"It looks like yours," she said.

"Lean forward," I instructed, and she did so I could gently pull the thick fabric over her head. I held the coffee so she could push her good arm through the sleeve and then watched as she slowly and gingerly pushed her newly bandaged arm into the shirt as well.

The grimace on her face made me angry at the asswipes in the other room all over again. When she was done, she sagged against the wall like she just completed a marathon.

After I got up from the cot and moved aside all the trash and supplies, I grabbed up a red Gatorade and took a long drink. I wondered what time it was, if it was fully dark yet, and how much longer we had until the cops showed up.

The situation didn't feel as urgent now that I was able to get her some medicine and really stop the bleeding. Still, she was in danger from her low body temperature and most likely dehydrated.

"There room on that thing for me?" I asked, nudging her good side.

She scooted over and I sat down, crowding her space and spreading my legs.

"Rude," Taylor said, scrunching up her nose and gesturing to the way I was making myself comfortable.

I grinned and reached for her. She made a little squeaking sound when I scooped her up and deposited her between my spread thighs and wrapped my arms loosely around her waist.

"Oh," she whispered.

"Oh?"

"You're incredibly warm."

"Soak it up, babe."

I guess I shouldn't have been surprised when she immediately sank farther into me, snuggling herself into the oversized sweatshirt and curling her body against mine.

But I was.

I was used to girls who liked to play games, who pretended to be hard to get.

Taylor turned so her injured arm was facing out and her opposite side leaned against me. Her head fit right in the space beneath my chin, and the scent of her shampoo wafted up my nose. I inhaled deep because it smelled so damn good.

So yeah, maybe my arm wound a little bit closer around her middle, and yeah, maybe I liked the way she fit against me. Like I was a puzzle with a missing piece, only I hadn't realized until it was fitted into place.

Once she was settled, I took the flannel and draped it over her. It wasn't much of a blanket, but it was all I had.

I was only doing this because of hypothermia. She was in danger.

I wasn't doing it because it made me want to throw her down on this cot and cover her body with mine. While we were both naked.

I wanted to ask her about herself, but I was afraid the guys would overhear. I didn't want them knowing anything extra about either one of us. So I didn't say anything. Really, it was better this way. It wasn't as if we were going to be friends after this. Getting to know her would just be a waste of time.

She tilted back her head, tipping up her chin, angling those emerald eyes at me. I couldn't help but look down. "I never realized being a criminal was so boring."

The chuckle rumbled deep in my chest, vibrating us both. "You mean getting shot wasn't enough excitement for you today?"

She smiled, flashing a row of white teeth. I liked when she smiled. I *really* liked when that smile was directed at me. "So is that what they do all day?" she whispered. "Hide?"

"Pretty much. They're like cockroaches… They only come out in the dark."

"Except today," she said, her voice turning a little dark. Taylor pulled her chin back down and pressed just a little closer. I rested my chin on top of her head, enjoying the feel of her silky strands against my unshaven face.

"Today kinda sucked." I agreed. I remembered the first time I was involved in something like this. The guys I was with wanted me to rob a gas station to prove I would do it.

So I did.

I pulled a black mask over my face, walked in, waved a gun around, and scared the shit out of an entire store of people. And then I stole some money, some booze, and a bag of chips.

(I was hungry and wanted chips.)

Unfortunately, the guy behind the counter wanted to be a hero. I gave him props silently, because defending what you considered yours was a natural instinct. It also showed the guy had some guts.

'Course, him being a pansy would have been a lot easier.

They were watching from the parking lot. He was challenging me with a loaded shotgun so I shot him.

I remember getting in the car, feeling it accelerate as we ripped down the road. I had to force those chips down the back of my throat. I had to sit there and eat like I was still hungry, like shooting that man for no reason didn't bother me at all.

It made me sick.

Sick with them, with myself.

I walked around for months wondering about that man, if he was alive or if I killed him. I walked around knowing that I shot him, knowing that if he died, it would be solely my fault. When I finally had a check-in with the PD several months later, the first thing I asked was about that man behind the register.

He hadn't died.

It didn't make me feel any better.

And that was just the start of my undercover career as a gangster. That was just the first instance in a long string of criminal activity in which I participated.

As time went on, it got easier. I found myself with a shorter fuse, more willing to rip into someone, more willing to get violent. I would tell myself that the scum deserved it, that he was a drug dealer or some lowlife who knocked up women only to bail on his responsibility.

I told myself that my actions were justified because I was doing it for the greater good, that in order to clean up the streets, someone had to get dirty.

And I got dirty… the kind of dirt that soap wouldn't wash away.

I knew exactly what Taylor was thinking right now. I knew her mind was trying to process this shitty, unexpected thing that happened. I knew she was likely trying to come up with a reason for it, trying to understand how something like this could just blow into an ordinary day and completely change everything.

People live inside their own little worlds, in the bubbles they create around themselves. Sure, they know bad things happen. They watch it on TV and see it on the news. But a lot of people, people like Taylor, never imagine it will come into their own backyard. They never think their entire life could flip so unexpectedly.

I knew it could.

I didn't want this for her.

I didn't want her to look in the mirror tomorrow and wonder what that bullet changed that she couldn't see. I didn't want her to remember the panic and fear of being held up in a place where she was supposed to be safe. I didn't want her to walk into every bank, every store and building, only to sweep her eyes around the room, looking for anything suspicious, looking for someone who might be concealing a gun.

It didn't matter what I wanted, because that's exactly what was going to happen.

Against me, she drew in a deep breath and slowly expelled it.

"You know I'm a really good palm reader." I lied.

I practically felt the darkest of her thoughts skitter away. "You read palms?" she asked, doubt heavy in her tone.

"Let me see your hand."

Taylor lifted her hand; it was completely concealed by the overly long sleeve of her hoodie. I chuckled and pulled it down, revealing slender, graceful fingers.

I cupped my hand around hers, pleased that it no longer felt icy cold, and turned it over so I could look into her palm.

I traced my fingers over the lines and curves in her skin. "Hmmm," I said. "This is very interesting."

She giggled.

I liked the way her skin felt in contrast to mine. Hers felt smooth and yielding, while mine seemed coarse and unforgiving. For a moment, I forgot I was supposed to be reading her palm and when I remembered, I tried to think of something that wouldn't sound completely idiotic.

What did the lines in the palm mean again?

She glanced up at me, curiosity in her eyes.

"This line here," I said, pointing to one of the deepest, longest lines, "is your life line."

"Well, my life line has blood on it," she said, amused.

I glanced down again and sure enough, toward the end was a splatter of blood. "That's not supposed to be there," I muttered and licked my thumb so I could wipe away the blood.

She giggled again and this time her laugh was strong enough that she wiggled against me. Desire spiked in my blood stream and something in the bottom of my stomach tightened a little bit.

I scrubbed away the blood and then held her hand out flat so I could study it anew. "It's a very long line," I murmured, starting at the base of her finger and lightly following the line down through the center of her palm and to the fleshy part near the base of her thumb.

"I guess that means I'm not going to die today," she said softly.

My arms locked up around her and I scooted her in toward my body just a little bit closer. I couldn't help but notice the way the roundness of her hip brushed right up against my cock. The pressure of her fitted against me was delicious.

"You are not dying here." I promised and rested the side of my cheek against her head. "This here"—I pointed, moving to another deep line in her palm—"is the…" I stuttered a little, grasping for something else to say.

"That's the love line," she filled in, her voice slightly wistful.

"Are you a palm reader too?" I asked, ducking my head to look at her in mock surprise.

She shook her head and rolled her eyes. "You are not a palm reader."

"Maybe not." I allowed. "Maybe, I just wanted to hold your hand."

She stilled, like she was replaying my words to make sure she heard them right. I enjoyed seeing the little bit of color seep into her cheeks before she ducked her head shyly. "You can," she said, holding out her hand once more.

All her fingers were pressed together, her palm facing me. It was more like she wanted to shake my hand. I brought my arm up and slid my palm against the back of her hand, wiggling my fingers between hers and curling them around, the tips caressing her palm.

She sighed, a contented little sound that made me feel like I just completed a marathon with the best time of all the runners, and her head fell against my chest.

Damn.

I wasn't used to this kind of physical contact. I was used to making out with girls I barely knew in darkened corners of bars or basements. I was used to copping feels and groping wherever my hands would reach. Oftentimes, me and the flavor of the night would drink enough to not care (but never enough to make me drop my guard) I didn't know her name. And then we would stumble somewhere more private and I would screw her without even thinking about it.

It was part of my cover. I was the guy who was too busy dicking around to pay too much attention to the business. I was the guy who would rather follow orders so I had more time with the ladies.

I didn't say I didn't like it. In my eyes, there was no such thing as bad sex. Sex felt good, it relieved stress, and yeah, the ladies were always willing.

And because they were always willing, I never had to put much effort into scoring. I never had to think about holding hands or making her smile. I never worried about if she was bored or worried about something.

But with Taylor, I did.

Having her in my lap, having her skin against my skin, feeling her steady, even breathing as she relaxed into my body… I wanted to hold her hand. I wanted to know what she was thinking, and I secretly hoped she enjoyed where she was sitting as much as I.

Is this what it was like to think about someone else ahead of yourself?

"Thank you," she whispered, drawing me out of my internal musings.

"For what?"

She lifted her head and looked up at me. God, I loved the way she looked at me. Like I fucking hung the moon or something. "For being here," she whispered. The side of her lip curved upward. "And for being so amazingly warm."

I tucked a strand of scarlet hair behind her ear and kissed her temple. "Drink your girly ass drink," I replied, gruff, handing her the bottle of purple Gatorade.

I leaned my head against the wall, thinking about how ape-shit crazy I was. This was a shitty, dangerous situation. I was supposed be on vacation right now, not patching up bullet wounds with stolen medical supplies.

Even so, there wasn't anywhere else I would rather be.

I heard a noise out by the couch but couldn't see around the corner. I heard a bit more scuffling and a couple low swears.

Every muscle in my body tensed.

Something was up.

And that something probably wasn't good. I needed to be out there solidifying my "relationship" with them. Selling them on the fact I was loyal to their cause. Hopefully, Mac and the rest of the people on the raid would be here soon, but until then, I needed to make sure this shit went smoothly.

The last thing we needed was something to go wrong.

"Why don't you lie down and rest," I murmured, lifting her against me and sitting up. Then I laid her gently on the cot.

"I was resting," she complained, that pouty lower lip poking out just a little bit more.

Shit, she was cute.

I used the flannel to cover her legs and then turned away to go see what the guys were up to. Snake was there, standing beside the hastily framed-out wall. The look on his face had everything inside me screaming red alert.

I stepped away from Taylor, keeping my body positioned between the cot and Snake. "What's up, man?"

He held up the smart phone in his hand. "You a fucking cop?" he said, his voice low and even. Violence radiated off his every pore.

Across the room, his three boys stood up in silent threat.

So much for shit going smoothly.

10

Taylor

I kept my body still, despite the barely contained turmoil sweeping through the room. I wanted to jump up and deny, deny, deny.

Cop? What cop? I wanted to ask, but I knew speaking would only make it worse. Surely Brody knew how to handle this kind of situation. Surely he could explain away whatever made them suspicious.

"You think I'm a cop?" Brody scoffed, his voice sounding slightly bemused. "That's actually pretty flattering. You think I could pull something like that off?"

My coiled insides relaxed slightly because he sounded so genuine there was no way they wouldn't believe him.

Snake laughed. "It's pretty out there."

I didn't like the way his laugh sounded. Slowly, I turned my head so I could look across the room. Brody's back was to me, and it blocked almost the entire view of Snake.

"Explain this," Snake snarled, and I saw his arm fling out as he thrust the phone at Brody.

Brody took the phone and held it in front of him. Several seconds later, I heard the audio begin to play. I recognized the music as the intro for a local news station here in Raleigh.

...The robbery of Shaw Trust earlier today has rocked the city of Raleigh. Despite the refusal of the local law enforcement to comment, Eye on Five managed to uncover some information on what turns out to be a very involved theft...

"What the hell is this?" Brody asked, cutting off the babbling of the news anchor.

"Watch it," Snake threatened, a gun appearing in his hand, pointed directly at Brody.

My breath caught and renewed fear took over my body. Once again, I found myself looking around the room for something I could use as a weapon. The audio filled the room once more and I listened as horror dawned.

...The only daughter of the prestigious Shaw family of Raleigh is said to have been in the bank at the time of the robbery and is now missing. We have learned from an unnamed source that surveillance footage shows Taylor Shaw being carried out of the bank, presumably against her will. Her father, Edward Preston Shaw, has put up a two million-dollar award for the safe return of his daughter...

Oh, this was bad.

...We have also learned that the man carrying her out of the building is police officer Brody West. Eye on Five learned his identity when his truck was left abandoned outside the bank and was eventually impounded by the very department he is said to work for.

Is this a case of good cop gone bad, or is there more to this case than meets the eye? We will keep you updated on this breaking case as details come in…

"I told you my name was Slater Bass. I don't know no Brody West," Brody said, handing the phone casually back to Snake.

How the hell could be be so calm?

They found him out! They found us out! I was literally trying not to scream like a hyena being chased by a lion (Do lions and hyenas even live in the same place?).

"You're telling me the news is wrong?" Snake asked.

"Well, they ain't right."

Snake looked down at the screen on his phone and, with a few swipes and taps of his fingers, brought up an image. He turned the screen around so it faced Brody. From my place on the cot, I could see it clearly.

It was a picture of Brody… in his police uniform.

My stomach heaved and the impulse to throw up all over everything was so strong I actually started to gag. Another tap on the screen brought up a picture of me from several years ago, with my father, standing in front of the bank.

I sat up, leaning against the wall. My arm protested when I moved, but it didn't hurt nearly as much as before. The numbing injections were still dulling the pain and the pain medicine was doing its job throughout my bloodstream.

Brody could have kept quiet back there at the bank. He could have let me lie there and bleed (like Brandy). If he had, then none of this would be happening right now. His cover would still be intact and I wouldn't be here.

I might be dead.

But maybe not. Maybe I would be at the hospital.

Either way, I couldn't just sit here and let them kill Brody for slipping under cover to help protect me. Yeah, I knew this was about more than me. It was about bringing these guys down. It was about returning the money that was stolen from my father's bank. I wasn't going to be a hindrance to Brody. I wasn't going to be some dead weight appendage that he had to drag around on his fight out the door. Injured or not, I was going to help him.

"You gonna deny it now?" Snake said, the other guys in the room taking a step closer to him.

I pushed up to my feet, swaying a little, like I just climbed off a boat and had a bad case of sea legs. I steadied myself and took a few steps toward Brody.

He tensed, the muscles in his back bunching. At his side and slightly behind him, he held up his palm, telling me to stop.

"It doesn't matter what I say," Brody replied. "Y'all have already decided what you believe."

"Before I kill you, I'm going to carve that tattoo out of your back and hang it in a frame for everyone to see what happens to those who disgrace this crew," Snake said, his voice oddly flat as he withdrew a knife out of the back of his pants.

A small sound of protest ripped from the back of my throat, and I couldn't stop myself from going to Brody's side. He held out his arm, tucking me behind him and using it as some sort of shield.

The tension in the room was so thick it was like smoke. It made it hard to breath and my eyes began to burn. Snake laughed, the sound doing nothing to dispel the heavy fog over us. His dark, callous eyes turned to me.

"Don't worry. We won't be killing you. We're going to need you for ransom."

"Ransom?" I asked, the fingers of my left hand coiling themselves into the belt loop of Brody's jeans.

"You're worth more to us alive than dead. How much do you think that rich Daddy of yours would be willing to pay to get you back?"

Revulsion hit me hard, like I was being hit head on by a car traveling at the highest speed. For a moment, I couldn't breathe. For a moment, my brain literally blanked out as I tried to process the hell my father would be put through.

And what was worse? He'd pay it. My father would pay whatever amount these immoral, disgusting pigs asked for. And he would get me back…

In a body bag.

I wasn't sure what to do. This kind of situation was beyond me; this was not something I ever in my life thought would happen. I was willing to fight like hell to get out of here, but I needed Brody to make the first move.

He was like a piece of carved granite in front of me. His entire body was solid and unmoving, so still that I might have been worried had I not been able to feel the heat coming off of his skin.

The room was incredibly silent while we all studied each other, waiting for someone to make the first move. I noticed the fingers on Brody's outstretched arm twitching ever so lightly. Snake put both the knife and his cell phone into one hand and then raised his gun with the other, pointing it directly at Brody's chest.

Brody's fingers twitched again. This time more insistent.

My fingers flexed around his belt buckle, agitated because I knew he was trying to tell me something. I just wasn't sure what it was.

And then my fingers brushed something hard.

I glanced down.

The gun.

Brody still had a gun and it was tucked in the waistband of his jeans. Just above my hand.

Moving fast, I yanked the gun free and pressed it into his waiting hand. He moved like a racehorse being let out of its starting gate, swinging the gun up and around in one second flat.

Snake gave a yell as Brody fired a single shot, but it hadn't been aimed at Snake.

The sound of glass shattering pierced the air and the room went black.

He shot out the lamp, the only source of light in this basement.

Snake fired a shot of his own, but Brody was already moving, diving to the side and yanking me with him. He tossed me against the nearby wall and my cheek bounced off the hard brick, but I didn't cry out. In order for us to get out of here, we had to be silent.

The only advantage we had was that it was dark and they couldn't see to shoot us.

Brody pressed his body along mine, sandwiching me between him and the wall. I felt his every contour; I even felt the rapid pounding of his heart.

He leaned down into my ear, speaking so low I barely heard his instructions. "Stay with me."

We inched along the wall while the sounds of scuffling and scurrying filled the room. Someone came close and Brody must have hit them because I felt him pull away, I heard a thud, and someone groaned.

I panicked, wanting to call out for him, terrified he might have been the one hit, but then his body found mine once more, shielding me and pulling me rapidly down the wall and toward the stairs.

I heard a little click and then a light pierced the deep blackness of the room. Someone turned on a flashlight app.

Fan-freaking-tastic.

"Move," Brody ordered as the bright beam found us. He shoved me toward the stairs and I stumbled.

"Fuck," he swore, scooping me back onto my feet and pushing me toward the bottom step. "Run, Taylor. Get the hell out of here and don't look back!"

I scrambled up the steps, only making it about halfway when I realized he wasn't right behind me.

"Brody!" I cried, turning back, looking for him.

He was planted at the bottom of the steps like some kind of badass bodyguard, brandishing a gun and holding them off.

As I stared, he raised the gun and fired off several shots in rapid succession.

"Run!" he yelled, not even looking up, but knowing I was there.

I started up the stairs again, but another shot had me turning back. I saw Brody jerk and stumble, reaching out to catch himself against the wall. Even as he fell, he fired his gun.

"Brody!" His name ripped from my throat as tears escaped from my eyes.

He grunted and got back to his feet, holding his side with one hand and firing with the other. I rushed back down the stairs. I couldn't leave him here. I couldn't let him stand there in harm's way so I could run.

He looked up. "No, Taylor. Get the hell out of here!"

"No!" I screamed, far enough down now I reached out and grabbed his arm to pull him up the stairs with me.

Another gun went off and I was knocked from my feet, landing brutally against the unforgiving wooden stairs, pain ricocheting throughout my entire body.

Brody wrapped his arm around me, pulling me into the security of his body as loud rumbling filled the tiny space. The stairs where I fell began to vibrate and shake. It was almost as if an earthquake were ripping through this tiny abandoned place.

Shouts and yelling erupted as things went from bad to worse.

11

Brody

There she goes again. Confusing the shit out of me.

I finally get the chance to get her out of here. I finally manage to get her to the stairs. So what does she do with the three-second window of escape I get her?

She runs back down the stairs toward me.

Damn, I knew I had a way with the ladies, but this was just excessive.

The only lighting came from one of those flashlight apps so there were definite shadows to disappear into, but it was hard to fool those gunning (literally) for us because we had to head toward the only exit in this place.

It became obvious as Taylor pulled on my arm, desperate to get to me follow, that I wasn't going to be able to stay behind to make sure she made it out first. She wasn't going to leave me behind.

As fucking frustrating as that was, it was also slightly endearing.

Most people in this life would shoot you, stampede over your body and then leave you there to rot if it got them somewhere. There wasn't much honor among thieves. There was a code, yeah. That's where the tattoo came in. But code went out the window when people were getting shot and there was a cop in the midst.

We only got about one step when I saw the gun being aimed through the bright flash of the light. I was rough when I threw her onto the steps and shielded her with my body, but having a few bruises was better than another bloody wound.

The bullet embedded itself in the block wall, inches above where we landed. A little bit of the wall crumbled and fell across the side of my face. God, that had been close.

Overhead, I heard men storming the building, vibrating the worn, thin floorboards above us. *Well, it's about fucking time,* I thought as the app shut itself off and we were once again plunged into absolute darkness.

Ignoring the sharp sting in my side and the warmth I felt running down beneath the waistband of my jeans, I scooped Taylor up, holding her against me as I practically dragged her up the stairs. Just as we reached the top, the door burst inward, shards of wood splintered everywhere, and I ducked over her, trying to shield her face.

"Raleigh PD!" a man roared from above, and an ultra-bright light shone down the stairwell, bathing everything in artificial white light.

I squinted against it and held up my hand. "It's West!" I yelled. "I have the hostage and I'm coming up!"

I hoped they were listening because I towed her up the rest of the way, rushing past what was left of the ancient door on its hinges. A bunch of scuffling and swearing could be heard from downstairs, and I glanced at the officer standing there, ready to go down.

"They have guns and have already used them." I warned and then pushed through the other ten or so officers who were standing there dressed in bulletproof vests, helmets, and gloves. All of them were armed with weapons and all of them meant business.

Orders were being shouted and footsteps rained down the stairs as we walked out of the gas station and into the parking lot, which was full of police cruisers and flashing lights.

Across the pavement was an ambulance, the lights on the top flashing in welcome.

"Over here!" I yelled, and the EMTs started toward us.

"I can walk," Taylor said, and I looked down, realizing I was still carrying her.

I stopped and let her slide down the side of my body until her feet touched the ground. "Were you hit again?" I asked, running my gaze over her body. It was dark, but I still noted the dark stain on the side of her hoodie.

"Shit!" I spat and grabbed at her, bringing her closer and yanking up the hem of the too-large sweatshirt. "Oh, Tay," I heard myself say. "I tried to shield you. I'm getting help right now," I said, frantic that she was shot again. If she lost any more blood tonight, she was going to be in serious danger.

I looked up, my eyes searching for the EMTs. Where the hell were they? She needed attention.

"Brody!" Taylor yelled, grabbing my face and forcing me to look at her. "Listen! I'm not shot. That isn't my blood."

It took a second for the pounding of my heart to let the words sink in, and when they did, I grabbed her by the waist and looked down again. "The blood—"

"The blood is yours," she said, covering my hands with hers.

I looked down at where the bullet grazed me earlier and noted the dark-red stain across my stomach and side. It lined up perfectly with the stain on her. The blood must have soaked into her clothes when I was carrying her.

"Thank God," I muttered, running a hand over the top of my head.

"Thank God?" She scoffed, looking at me like I was insane. "You're relieved that you got shot?"

"I'd take ten bullets if it meant you didn't have to take any." The truth just burst right out of my mouth, shocking the shit out of both of us. I knew I was attracted to her. I mean, shit, she was hot as hell. But that comment… that comment made me wonder if maybe I felt something more toward her than just sexual attraction.

Taylor's lips parted and her eyes widened. Both of us stood there with blood on our clothes, wounds in our bodies, and exhaustion under our eyes. Yet I couldn't feel any of it.

The EMTs chose that moment to arrive and separate us, each of them looking us over and assessing our injuries. I brushed off the man's hands when he tried to look under my shirt. "I'm fine. It's her that needs the medical attention."

"Don't listen to him," Taylor called. "He was shot!"

"Eh, it just grazed me."

"That's a lot of blood for a drive-by," the EMT said, referring to the fact I claimed the bullet just nicked me on the way past.

"Ma'am…" The other EMT sighed loudly, and I looked up to see Taylor with a stubborn set to her jaw.

"What's wrong?" I asked, my eyes narrowing on the EMT. If he hurt her…

"She's refusing to get in the ambulance," the guy replied.

I looked at Tay for confirmation, lifting my eyebrows.

"I'm not going unless you let them look at you too."

High maintenance. That's what she was.

"Fine," I sighed and followed behind them all toward the ambulance. Behind me, the sounds of gunfire erupted, along with some shouting and sounds of a scuffle.

I spun, catching sight of someone sprinting off around the side of the building. It was Snake. He was attempting to flee the scene. Three officers took off after him. I considered running him down myself. I wanted to see him behind bars more than anyone here.

Just as I took a step in his direction, a small, cool hand wrapped around mine. "Please don't," she whispered.

I looked down at where she grasped my hand and then back up at her fear-filled face. There was blood smeared on her cheek.

"C'mon," I said, pulling my hand away to swing my arm over her shoulder. As we walked toward the back of the lit ambulance, I couldn't help but look back at where Snake disappeared.

"West," a familiar voice said from behind. It was Mac, my superior and the man who burst in here tonight.

"Timing couldn't have been better," I said.

"Well, we wouldn't have been able to make this bust at all if it wasn't for you."

Behind us, one of the EMTs sighed loudly. "Ma'am, we need to get you started on fluid immediately."

"You are not sticking me with that needle." Taylor refused.

"Quit being a pain in the ass, Tay," I called.

She glared at me.

I turned back to the chief. He raised his brow at me. I shrugged. "She's high maintenance."

"Are you speaking about my daughter?" someone with a deep voice said from behind.

I spun and glanced at a tall man with salt-and-pepper hair, lines at the corners of his eyes, and dressed in a navy-blue suit complete with a tie.

"Mr. Shaw," Mac said, stepping forward. "Your daughter is safe. She's being treated right now." Mac pointed to where Taylor was sitting in the back of the ambulance.

Mr. Shaw's eyes glanced over to his daughter but then came quickly back to mine. "Are you the man who kidnapped my daughter?"

"I'm the man that kept her alive."

His haughty, all-assuming tone did not work on me. Please. I used to live in the ghetto; his suit and money hardly intimidated me.

"Ow!" Taylor howled from behind and I tensed, spinning around, afraid Snake had managed to work his way around the perimeter of the land and come for her.

Snake was nowhere to be seen, but she was sitting in the back of the ambulance sort of hunched over on herself and the EMT was standing over her, scowling.

Like a rubber band stretched way too far, something in me snapped. I stepped around a few people that were milling about and approached where Taylor was sitting inside along a narrow bench that ran the length of the vehicle.

"What's the matter?" I asked, putting a hand on her shoulder and drawing her upward so I could see what she was hunched around.

The back of her hand was bleeding, a thin rivulet of blood trailing over the thin, pale skin and disappearing around to her palm.

"He stabbed me with a needle!" she accused, glancing at me with wet eyes and then glaring at the man.

Seeing her bleeding yet again really, really pissed me off. Before I could think twice, I plowed into the man, charging him backward and ramming him into the side of the car. I pinned him with my forearm up against the side and looked into his face.

"She's been shot, kidnapped, and traumatized, and you stab her with a goddamn needle?" I growled.

The man's eyes widened and I knew I looked rather scary, with my bloody hands and clothes and the wild look I knew was swimming in my eyes. "I didn't mean to!" he protested. "She wouldn't hold still."

"West," Mac said from right beside me. "What the hell are you doing?"

I blew out a breath and felt some of the initial panic and anger I felt at seeing her blood ebb away. I dropped the man and he collapsed onto his ass on the bench beneath him. "No, fucking bedside manner," I muttered and strode the short distance toward Taylor.

She was still cradling her hand in her lap, her hair was tangled, her clothes were dirty, bloody, too big and her lips were dry and cracked.

I dropped down on my haunches in front of her and picked through the small kit off to the side. I reached for her hand and she gave it willingly, not even uttering a word of protest. I cleaned off the blood, wiping it away and watching as a bead of fresh new blood welled to the surface. I covered it with a small piece of gauze and then picked up the IV, which the asshole was trying to put in the back of her hand.

"Want me to kiss it and make it better?" I asked softly, speaking only to her. Those jewel-like eyes glanced up away from her hand and fastened onto me.

Without waiting for her reply (like she'd say no), I lifted her hand and pressed my lips near the area I was applying pressure to. Before pulling back, I let my tongue glide over her in a single caress and was rewarded with a spattering of goose bumps racing up her arm.

As I lowered her hand I felt her eyes on me once more and I took advantage of the moment to gently slide the new IV into place.

She winced and I squeezed her fingers. "All done."

After I tossed aside the bloody gauze, I applied fresh padding and some medical tape to the back of her hand to hold the IV in place. "Don't move around too much," I told her. "The more you do, the more it will tug on your skin."

"Thanks," she said, giving me a little smile as I returned her hand to her lap. I stood up and, without thinking, leaned down and pressed a kiss to the center of her forehead.

The silence around us seemed rather penetrating so I glanced around. Mac, Mr. Shaw, a couple EMTs, and a few cops were all standing there watching us with their mouths slackened.

"What?" I bellowed. Throats cleared and people started moving around again.

They acted like me being nice was some sort of miracle, like I was usually akin to a caveman with a bad case of monkey butt.

Okay, yeah… that might be accurate.

"Taylor," Mr. Shaw said, brushing past me like I was some piece of garbage on the street.

"Dad!" she said, and I heard the relief in her tone. I guess if she loved him I would try not to deck him.

"You get them all?" I asked Mac, stepping down from the back of the ambulance.

"All of them but one."

"Snake is still gone?" I should have gone after him. He was the mind behind this whole thing; he was the one that would do something like this again.

"His name is Snake?" Mac asked.

"That's what he said."

"I need you to come down to the station so we can get all your knowledge into a statement."

Movement around the building paused our conversation and we watched several officers coming out with the large bags full of cash.

"Yeah, I figured," I said. "Let's go." I motioned toward one of the black unmarked sedans.

"Wait," Taylor called, and I looked back. "He needs to come to the hospital!"

Mac looked at me with a shrewd gaze. He sighed. "Is that your blood, West?" he asked, looking at my shirt.

"It's not that bad," I lamented.

"Go," he ordered.

I was about to protest, but he held up his hand. "Just freaking go. If you don't, the department head will be breathing down my ass for weeks."

I didn't protest too much. I'd lost more blood than I wanted to admit, and I was feeling a little lightheaded.

"I'll meet you at the hospital after we wrap this up here," Mac said before turning away to issue orders.

I climbed into the back of the ambulance, sitting across from Taylor and her father.

"Maybe I should ride with you," her father said, glancing at me.

What a jackass.

"No, Dad," she sighed. "I'm fine and you have your car here."

He turned toward her. "I'll be at the hospital when you get there."

"Okay."

His eyes softened when he looked at her, and some of the animosity I felt toward him disappeared. He must not be that bad if he loved her, and it was clear he did. "I'm so glad you're okay."

She smiled. "Me too."

When he was gone, the EMTs glanced at us warily. "We'll be fine back here alone."

They didn't argue, instead eagerly shutting us in the back and then jumping into the front of the cab.

"What did you do to those poor guys?" I asked Taylor.

She laughed. "What a bunch of wieners."

A laugh burst from my throat and my side stung. "Did you just call them wieners?"

"If the shoe fits…" She shrugged.

I grinned.

"Hey," she said softly after a moment.

The vehicle began moving forward and the lights from the scene faded away.

"Yeah?"

"Thanks for everything."

"Just doing my job," I said casually, even as my insides felt anything but.

Nothing at all about the way I felt for Taylor was casual.

12

Taylor

Just doing my job.

If he said those words one more time, I might scream.

Maybe I would feel differently in the morning. After I was safe in the hospital, with pain meds dulling the sharp ache in my body, but until then, no. Just no.

Until then, I didn't want to hear this was only a job for him. I didn't want to hear that the reason it felt so good to be tucked up close to him was because I was in a dangerous and traumatic situation. I didn't feel traumatized.

I felt... I felt like I liked being near him.

I wanted to sit here in the back of this ambulance, reliving the moment he kissed me, reliving the gentle way he tried to take away the sting of the IV. I wanted to romanticize the totally pissed look on his face when he saw the blood on my hand from that total douche bag of an EMT.

Yeah, I wasn't in high school and I shouldn't be over here swooning, especially since I almost died, but I couldn't help it. I couldn't help feeling like there was more between us than some sort of bond that we forged when he was saving my life.

I didn't want him to say he was just doing his job. I wanted him to say the thought of me being hurt drove him insane. That even though we didn't know each other, the thought of never seeing me again was too much to bear.

Yeah, so maybe I was a sappy romantic.

I almost died. I'm entitled to excessive daydreaming about a ripped, tattooed cop who doesn't think twice about firing a gun and throwing a punch.

I'd take ten bullets if it meant you didn't have to take any.

Sigh

Okay, that was way better than anything I just imagined. And he actually said that.

"What's wrong?" he said, gazing across the inside of the ambulance with a concerned look on his face.

I must have sighed out loud.

"Nothing," I answered. I couldn't help but notice the dark stain on his shirt. "But you haven't even been looked at."

Worry struck me. He'd been so busy insisting I get taken care of and then looking after me that no one bothered to take care of him. I felt like an ass.

Worse than an ass. I felt like a turd circle.

Nearby, there was a little kit one of the EMTs left out, and I grabbed it and stepped toward him. Of course, the ambulance chose that moment to stop abruptly. The guy driving laid on the horn, and I was sent flying sideways.

Brody moved fast, reaching out to steady me, and then the ambulance started moving again, throwing us both into the seat.

"These guys are complete idiots," he muttered.

I was half reclining across his chest, lying between his legs. He seemed to realize I was lying on him and he looked down. "What'cha doing over here?" he asked softly.

"Someone needs to look at your side." I breathed, proud that I actually remembered.

His fingers brushed through the hair at the side of my head. "Here I thought maybe you just missed me."

"Maybe I did," I admitted.

He leaned down and I moved up, both of us meeting in the middle. Our mouths brushed together and Brody's fingers tightened around the back of my head, holding me close so he could deepen the kiss.

This time, instead of catching my bottom lip between his, he nibbled at my top lip, applying a little bit of pressure as he pulled it out and nipped at it. As much as I loved the heated, playful gesture, I wanted more. I wanted to feel his tongue against mine. I wanted to feel him move inside me.

I pushed myself closer and his hand left the back of my head and wound around my waist, anchoring me against him as he dragged me upward so he would have better access to my lips.

Anticipation curled my toes as we kissed again, this time full on the mouth, neither of us pulling back, just enjoying the constant rubbing together of our lips. If he kissed me any harder, I was sure sparks would ignite and we might start a fire. I grabbed his side, wanting him even closer, wanting his tongue, practically begging for it.

He winced but didn't pull away, kissing me through the pain.

"I'm sorry," I said, finally disconnecting our lips, glancing down at the place I grabbed. The place he was shot.

I tried to push up off him so I could sit back and see if I did any damage, but he growled and pulled me back. "I'm not done kissing you yet," he rumbled.

I giggled and surrendered willingly. The feel of him against me was too much to fight. When our lips connected once more, his hips surged upward and I felt his hard length straining against his jeans. It pushed against me, and I gasped.

He took the moment to sweep his tongue into my wide-open mouth, and I groaned. Oh my goodness, it felt like heaven. No, wait. It felt like sin. Delicious sin that would turn even an angel into an outlaw.

His tongue was thick and wide, taking over the inside of my mouth and lapping at my own with force and command. It slid past my teeth and spun around, almost like it was inviting my tongue to dance.

My body went slack in his arms, completely compliant to him and the spell he cast over me. I didn't care if yielding made me weak… because I was. The driving force of his broad, insistent tongue turned me into nothing but a puddle of desire, and all I could think about was where else his tongue might travel.

We were so far gone in the each other's arms that neither of us noticed the ambulance come to a stop. In fact, I barely heard the backdoors being opened, and I didn't blink at the way the night air rushed over my flushed skin.

Brody grasped my face in his hands and pulled back, looking at me like we didn't have an audience, like I was the only thing he saw.

"You still taste damn good," he whispered, his voice husky with desire.

The IV line sticking out of my hand was tangled around him, and instead of pulling away quickly, knowing we'd been caught making out, he untangled himself with slow and deliberate ease, taking care not to cause me any extra pain.

The EMTs were amused when we made our way to the back of the ambulance, and when one of them reached up to help me out, Brody brushed him aside and reached in, lifting me and the portable IV out, anchoring me at his side.

"Lead the way," he said to the men who could only stare.

Finally, they moved off toward the emergency exit and Brody nudged me along behind them.

As we were walking between the sliding doors and across the threshold into the chaotic ER, Brody leaned close, his breath fanning out over my ear and causing little ripples of longing to race across my skin.

"I'd get shot all over again for another kiss like that."

I pressed my still-tingling lips together and smiled. So would I.

13

Brody

As I knew, my wound wasn't all that serious. The bullet grazed me on the way past, ripping the top layer of flesh and damaging some tissue on its way. It bled more than it should have, but that's because right after it happened I threw us onto the stairs, ripping the skin farther, and then carried Taylor out of the building.

Once it was cleaned and wrapped, the doctor told me I could go and tried to give me a prescription for pain pills. I left the script lying on the bed. I didn't take drugs, even if they were only pain pills.

There were times when I was undercover that I had to, and I knew how easily it was to jones for the next fix, to look for that high. I wasn't an addict and I never planned on being one. If I needed drugs to get through the pain of this wound, then I was a damn pussy.

I walked down the hall toward Taylor's room. The nurse tried to tell me I wasn't allowed to see her ('cause I wasn't family), but I ignored her and kept walking. If they wanted to keep me out of that room, they could call security.

I smirked.

Security wouldn't be able to keep me out either.

She must have realized because she didn't even call after me as I walked away. Maybe she recognized the look of a determined man. Determined and exhausted. God, this had been a long fucking day.

I knew I had to get to the station; a mountain of paperwork was waiting for me. But I couldn't leave until I checked on Taylor. I had to make sure the treatment I gave her while we were in that basement didn't do more harm than good.

I didn't knock when I arrived at her private room; I just pushed open the door and stepped inside. She was lying in a hospital bed, white blankets covering her past her waist. Her red hair was laid out across the pillow and her lashes were swept down against her pale cheeks. I never really noticed before how fine-boned she seemed, how fragile. But looking at her now made my stomach tighten into a hard knot as I thought about everything she went through earlier today.

She was hooked up to several monitors and of course an IV, and I glanced down at her hand to make sure it was taped up securely.

Her father was reclining in a nearby chair, his feet flat on the floor and his tie slightly askew. I wasn't sure how old he was, but I would place him in his fifties. I wondered where her mother was… why she wasn't keeping vigil beside her as well.

I took a step closer and Mr. Shaw stirred, opening his eyes and staring directly at me. I looked back, not necessarily challenging him, but not willing to back down either. I had a feeling this guy was used to getting what he wanted and people running to do his bidding. I wasn't one of those people and he needed to know that.

"What are you doing in here?" he asked.

Wasn't it obvious? "Checking on Taylor."

"Wasn't there a guard at the door?"

"Nope." Although, I liked the idea of there being one.

He frowned and sat up, looking at his watch. "He should have been here an hour ago."

"Might want to get someone more reliable. Taylor needs better protection than that."

He regarded me coolly. "I agree."

"Why don't you go get some coffee, make a phone call, and fire the putz who didn't show up?"

"You trying to get rid of me?" he asked.

"I wasn't aware I needed to."

We stared at each other once more, sizing each other up without saying a word.

Taylor shifted in the bed and made a small sound. Since I was already on my feet, I made it to her side before her father (which I took a little too much pleasure in) and rested my hand on the edge of her bed.

She looked up, her jade eyes focusing on me, and then she smiled. "Hey."

That smile had the ability to melt icecaps. It certainly took away the sting of the wound in my side. "Hey."

Her eyes ran over my face. "How are you? Why aren't you lying down?"

I chuckled. It was cute she thought I needed to lie down. A naughty comeback surfaced on the tip of my tongue about where I wanted to lie down, but I kept it in. I didn't think her father would appreciate my impure thoughts.

"They released me."

She wrinkled her nose. "They're making me stay overnight."

From the foot of the bed, Mr. Shaw cleared his throat. "Do you need anything, honey? Should I get the nurse?"

"I'm fine, Dad," she said, giving him a reassuring smile. "Have you been sleeping in the chair?"

"Of course."

"You don't have to stay. It's so late. I know you must have a million things to do."

"Nothing as important as you."

Was it possible to be jealous of a parent? It seemed wrong to be mad about the way she smiled tenderly at him. Knowing that being jealous was stupid didn't make me feel it any less.

"Taylor, honey, do you mind if I just step out to get some coffee? Make a call?" he asked.

"Of course not."

Mr. Shaw glanced at me.

"Oh," Taylor said, looking between us. "I didn't introduce you. Dad, this is Brody West. He was the police officer who bandaged my wound and pretty much kept me alive." She turned to me. "Brody, this is my dad, Edward Shaw."

"I know who he is," Edward replied.

"Dad," she groaned. "Really?"

He stepped around me to kiss the top of Taylor's head and then turned to me. I could see the struggle in his eyes. He wanted to ask me, but at the same time he didn't want to.

"I'll stay until you come back." I offered, giving the man a break. His kid was in the hospital after all.

He nodded once and exited the room quietly.

I looked down to see her fingers spider-crawling across the crappy hospital blanket toward mine. She hesitated, but then a single finger stretched out toward where mine rested on the mattress. I met her halfway, slipping my fingers between hers.

"Are you really okay?" she asked, staring at our joined hands.

I caught the leg of the chair her father had been sitting in and dragged it closer, pulling it up right beside the bed to sit down. Before I lowered myself, I lifted up the torn and bloody shirt and showed her the fresh, clean bandage wrapped around my waist. "The bullet just grazed me."

She blew out a breath like she had been nervous.

"How about you?" I asked, sitting down but keeping hold of her hand. I liked the way it felt in mine.

"The doctors were really impressed with your stitch job. They didn't even redo it. They re-bandaged it, gave me a couple more shots…" She paused to stick out her tongue. "And strapped me in this sling."

I glanced at the white sling holding her arm against her body. "They give you any good meds?"

She giggled and I took that as a yes. "Where else are you hurt?" I asked, concerned. I hadn't been gentle when I threw her onto those stairs when we were being shot at. I knew I probably hurt her, but I couldn't be sorry.

"Nothing major. A couple cuts and bruises."

"Like this one," I said, pulling my hand away from hers and lightly touching the side of her cheek where Snake hit her at the bank.

He was still at large. The police had an APB out for his arrest.

"Nothing a little makeup won't fix." Taylor pulled my hand away from the bruise and threaded her fingers through mine once more. "You're a good hand holder."

I grinned. "You think so?"

She nodded. "You fold your fingers around mine, like really tangle us together. It's like you want to touch me."

I did want to touch her. I wanted to touch more than just her hand. "Isn't this the way everyone holds hands?" I asked.

She shook her head. "Every other guy I dated never intertwined our fingers. He always just kind of cupped my hand in his." She made a face. "It was lame."

"Sounds like you've dated a lot of guys," I said, irritation clouding my tone. I didn't want to think of anyone else's hands on her.

"Not really. A few. My father runs most of them off."

Suddenly her father didn't annoy me as much.

She made a little sound. "I didn't mean to imply that we're dating," her cheeks flamed a shade that matched her hair. "Obviously, we aren't… I just meant—"

"I know what you meant." I grinned. I liked seeing her flustered.

"Will you hand me that water?" she asked, pulling back her hand.

I gave her the cup and watched her lips wrap around the striped straw. Once she had her fill, she lowered it and studied me. "Did they catch him?"

I knew she was asking about Snake. "No. He disappeared. But they're still looking."

Fear clouded her eyes.

[123]

"You're safe," I told her, taking the cup and setting it aside. I didn't want her to be afraid. "They'll get him soon."

"So what now?" She leaned her head back against the pillow and looked at me.

"You get some rest and I get to do paperwork."

"How long have you been a police officer?"

"About six years."

"You've been in lots of dangerous situations before?"

"A few." I hedged. My entire career was pretty much one big dangerous situation, but whatever.

"That tattoo," she began. "The one on your back. It marks you as part of a gang?"

"Yeah. It was part of my cover for the last case I worked on."

"Seems extreme to have to carry around a gang symbol for life for a temporary job."

I shrugged. "The job might have been temporary, but it's part of me now. Besides, I earned that tattoo."

She nodded. I don't think she knew what to say to that. I didn't mean to make it sound like I was proud of things I'd done to get this tattoo… Of course, I wasn't ashamed either. I wasn't like the men she was probably used to. I wasn't black or white. I was the kind of guy who existed in the gray area of life… in between the bad and the good, kind of stuck being pulled in both directions.

She yawned, revealing her little pink tongue, and my blood pressure started to rise. "Why don't you get some sleep?" I told her gruffly, remembering the way it felt to invade her mouth with mine.

"I'm glad you came by," she said, her voice already drowsy.

I didn't respond, but I did prop my boots up on the side of the bed and make myself comfortable. The papers at the station could wait. Silence settled over the room and I closed my eyes, thinking longingly of the hat I lost in the basement. It was always good for shading my eyes when I wanted to catch a few Z's. I didn't really want to leave. I liked sitting here with her. It was comfortable... It felt right.

Sleep wasn't hard to find. In fact, it claimed me rather quickly. Unfortunately, it wasn't as easy to keep. The earlier events made me a little twitchy. I'd learned to become a light sleeper because sleeping in a house full of drug addicts and criminals was never a good place to let down my guard. Add that to the fact I had been shot and threatened just hours before, and you could say I was extra... cautious.

Okay, pissed off was more the term.

The door to her room creaked open and the sound of light footfalls approaching the bed stirred me awake. I didn't move a muscle, just stayed reclined in the chair, listening. It was almost like they were creeping into the room, toward us, and it made the hair on the back of my neck stand tall.

The person stepped around me, avoiding my chair. I felt rather than saw the person reach out toward the precarious tubing leading straight into Taylor's hand. I reacted swiftly, snatching the hand out of midair, stopping them from taking hold of her tubing. The chair I was sitting in skidded back across the room and hit the wall when I jumped up out of it and pulled the intruder up against my body, pinning them with my arms.

"What the hell do you think you're doing?" I growled low.

A small whimper escaped, and I blinked, fully taking in the situation. A woman dressed in blue scrubs was rigid and breathing heavily up against me.

"Shit," I muttered, releasing her gently. "I'm sorry," I told the nurse. "I was asleep and you startled me."

"I tried not to wake you," she said, looking at me warily and taking a step back.

"Yeah." I scrubbed a hand down my face. "Sorry, I'm a little jumpy today."

The nurse softened. "That's understandable."

"Brody?" Taylor asked, looking between me and the nurse. Her eyes were wide and I wasn't sure if she saw what happened or not.

"Nurse just came in to check on you."

"I'm just going to check the fluid here and the IV," she explained, looking at me and not Taylor.

I nodded and she did her job quickly. After making sure Taylor was comfortable, she hurried toward the door.

"Mr. Shaw," she said cordially, slipping past Taylor's dad who was standing in the doorway.

I wondered how long he'd been there.

"Everything okay?" Taylor asked him.

He was carrying a white Styrofoam cup with steam coming from the top. "Absolutely," he said, smiling down at her.

"I gotta get to the station," I said, wanting to get down there to see if they brought in Snake yet. Besides, if the nurse hadn't been calling for security before, she probably was now.

Taylor focused those big green eyes on me. "You have to leave?"

It was very satisfying to hear the disappointment in her tone. Ignoring her father, I leaned down, caging her in with both my arms, and let my eyes wander over her features one last time. She really was a beautiful woman. "Take care of yourself," I whispered and kissed her on the forehead.

The little sigh I received was almost just as good as a full-on kiss.

"Bye," she whispered, watching me go.

"Mr. Shaw," I said as I passed Edward, who was standing there watching us with a displeased look on his face.

Poor guy, he probably wasn't used to someone not caring what he thought.

A few steps down the hall, he called out my name behind me. I stopped and pivoted around. "Yeah?"

"I'd like to speak to you a moment," Edward said.

I joined him beside the door to Taylor's room without saying a word.

"I saw what you did to that nurse," he said, getting right to the point.

"She caught me off guard." I shrugged. I wasn't going to apologize to him for reacting in a defensive way. I had a right to protect myself and those that belonged to me.

Whoa. *Those that belonged to me.* That was just a tad possessive, even for me. Maybe there was something in that shot the nurse forced on me.

"She was reaching for my daughter," he said, like he was telling me something I didn't know.

"And?"

"And your instinct was to protect her."

I stared at him in stony silence. Was he pissed that I was protective of his daughter?

"I'd like to hire you," he said. It was the second time in the span of ten minutes I was caught off guard.

"I don't have any experience in finances," I said. "I'm a cop."

"I have all the employees I need at my bank." He waved away my words.

"About that." I interrupted. "One of your associates literally stepped over your bleeding daughter to get the hell out of the building. Even after Taylor protected her." I crossed my arms over my chest, getting pissed all over again just thinking about it.

"Who?" he said coolly.

I shrugged.

"I'll take care of it." He spoke like it was a done deal, and I had no doubt that woman was going to be fired. "I want to hire you to protect my daughter."

I couldn't help but be surprised. "You want to what?"

"Obviously, the people I hire are complete morons. The guard in the bank couldn't thwart the robbery. The guard I hired to be here outside her room never showed... Apparently even when you have money, reliable help is hard to find."

"Money just makes it harder to find trustworthy employees."

"You're right." Edward agreed. "I may not like you much, but it's clear you have a softness for my daughter."

He didn't like me. Big fat fucking deal. But the fact he seemed to pick up on the way I felt for Taylor made me a little uncomfortable. I wasn't used to having *softness*. "I'm not a bodyguard," I replied. "I work for the RPD."

"I'm sure I could arrange to borrow you from the force."

"Do you always throw money around to get what you want?" I asked.

"When it comes to my daughter's safety, yes."

I studied him.

"She told me about the plan of using her for ransom. One of the thieves is still out there. What are the odds he will come back for her?"

I wished I could say I thought Snake would turn tail and get the hell out of town, but I knew better. I knew these guys were territorial. He wasn't going to just cut and run. Especially now that he knew I'm a cop and was responsible for thwarting his grand plans of being the next kingpin in the organization. "It's a possibility."

"Be at this address early the day after tomorrow morning. The police are putting a man outside the door here until she is discharged tomorrow evening. She's staying with me, and I have a very early day at the bank. This breech in security is making our members very antsy." He handed me a business card with what I assumed was his home address.

"I didn't say I would do it."

"It's just until this criminal is captured." He just kept talking like he hadn't heard me at all. "Then, I will be happy to not see you again."

Wow, he was really laying on the charm to get me to agree.

"I'll give you one hundred thousand dollars."

Surprise shot through me like a bullet. A hundred grand for what would likely be a day or two of work? Damn.

A rapid beeping sound floated through the door, and then Taylor cried out. Both of us barreled into the room. The first thing I did was sweep the space with my eyes, and my arm went to my back, reaching for my gun.

The gun wasn't there.

She made another sound of distress and my feet skidded across the linoleum as I rushed to her bedside. "Taylor," I called, leaning over her, taking her hand. She was having a nightmare.

She gasped, her eyes flying open and her body jerking upright.

"Easy," I murmured, catching her gently by the shoulders to keep her from flailing about too much and hurting herself.

"Brody?" she asked, her unfocused eyes seeking me out. When she saw I was there, she gave a cry of relief and flung herself at me, her free arm wrapping around my neck as she buried her face in my chest.

A tidal wave of fierce protectiveness swept over me. The fact that she willingly rushed into my arms for comfort heightened a primal need within me. I wanted to protect her. I wanted to be the one to soothe her when she was upset.

"It was just a bad dream," I said softly, splaying my hand against her back and pulling her a little bit closer.

"Please don't leave," she whispered.

"I'm not going anywhere."

The phone in Edward's pocket went off, shattering the quiet in the room. Taylor jolted in my arms and I glanced at Edward, who was letting it ring while he stared at us with an unreadable expression on his face.

"If you aren't going to get that, at least shut it the hell off," I growled.

He pulled the phone out and looked at the screen. He sighed. "I have to get this."

[130]

I waved him away and he answered, stepping out of the room and pulling the door around behind him.

I sat down on the edge of the bed, keeping my arm around her. She practically crawled into my lap, and I chuckled. "You're going to hurt your arm and pull out your IV."

"I don't care." Her voice was muffled against my shirt.

"Lie down," I ordered, pushing her into the covers.

I saw the flash of defiance in her eyes, but then I kicked my legs up on the bed and scooted up beside her (careful of the IV) and she decided not to refuse.

"Come here," I murmured, opening my arm. Her body fit right up against me and I turned so I was on my side, facing her, with my arm draped over her middle.

I could tell she wanted to turn as well, to push that ass of hers right up against my hips, but the sling and monitors would not allow it. Instead, she turned her face so it was buried in my neck.

She didn't say anything, but the slight tremble in her body faded away and she released a contented sigh before slipping back into a deep slumber.

I sat there a long time, not sleeping, just feeling her against me. I wasn't used to this kind of shit. I was used to wham-bam-thank-you-ma'am. I wasn't used to holding hands, kisses that didn't lead to sex, and a woman who acted like I was the cure for everything that ailed her.

I liked it.

I was dozing off when Edward came back into the room. He stopped short when he noticed I was in the bed and she was plastered against my side.

I glanced up at him, speaking softly above Taylor's sleeping head. "I'll do it," I said, accepting the job.

He nodded.

"One thing," I said.

"What?"

"I don't want your money."

Surprise flickered in his eyes. "You're turning down payment?"

"Yes." I had money of my own. I didn't want or need his.

I wanted something else from him.

I wanted his daughter.

14

Taylor

My father left early, and as soon as I got out of bed, I told his housekeeper she could take the day off. I didn't want or need a babysitter.

Time alone sounded pretty nice, though. People were hovering around me since I was admitted in the hospital. My father, the nurses, the doctor, the police officer at the door. I was constantly surrounded. Sometimes I went into the bathroom just to hide. All these people… and not one of them were who I really wanted. After Brody left that night, he hadn't been back. I understood he had work to do and a life of his own, but every time the door to my room opened, my heart would leap, hoping it was him. And when it wasn't, disappointment burned the back of my throat.

Was it possible to become attached to someone through a life-altering situation? Was it possible to develop real feelings for someone under circumstances of duress? Or was Brody just someone whose memory would fade over time?

The thought scared me. I barely knew him, but I wanted the chance to change that.

My entire body was like one giant ache as I moved through the rooms of my father's too-big house, not really looking at anything, but just moving, just trying to work out some of the soreness.

Of course, this wasn't like a pulled muscle. This wasn't like I ran one too many miles at the gym the day before. I couldn't just walk off the soreness of being shot and almost killed. I wasn't sleeping well because I was plagued with dreams of gunfire, money, and basements without windows.

It would take time for some of my fear to wear away. I understood that and I was okay with it. But a little bit of peace might be nice.

What I needed was a soak in a warm bath. Reversing my path through the house, I walked toward the stairs and on my way through the entryway, someone knocked on the door. I froze, my foot on the bottom step, as I wondered who it could be.

Fear skittered up my spine as I imagined the worst. It was probably Snake, who somehow evaded the police and could be anywhere by now. *Get real,* I admonished myself. It wasn't as if he would walk up to my door in broad daylight and knock.

Knock, knock.

Who's there?

I've come to finish what I started.

I shook my head of the silly, far-fetched thought while I backtracked to the door. "Who is it?" I called out. I might be acting paranoid, but it was better safe than sorry.

"It's Brody." His voice was like a warm breeze on a cold day. Unexpected but entirely welcome.

I yanked open the door, sunshine climbing across the floor and warming my chilly toes. But I didn't notice the heat or the sun. I didn't notice the blue sky behind him or anything else that might be out there. He was all I saw. He commanded my attention like a bolt of lightning across a dark and stormy sky.

He was dressed in a pair of ratty, faded blue jeans. The tears in the fabric showed little glimpses of his skin and the worn-out fabric molded to his thighs like a lover. His hunter-green T-shirt looked like combed cotton, or perhaps it had just been washed over and over again. It wasn't overly snug, but the sleeves clung to his defined biceps and tattoos stretched down his arms. Shielding his eyes was a pair of aviator glasses, and by the look of his jaw, I was sure he hadn't shaved.

"Hey," I said, my voice sounding slightly breathless. "I didn't expect to see you."

The corner of his mouth lifted and even though I couldn't see his eyes, I knew he was staring at me. I could feel the heat of his gaze. "That mean I can't come in?"

I pushed the door open wide. "Of course you can."

"How's the arm?" he asked, strolling inside with his hands casually tucked in his pockets.

"Not so bad." In truth, it hurt less than the rest of me.

He chuckled. "You're sore as hell, aren't you?"

I groaned. "Yep."

"It'll fade," he said softly, sliding the sunglasses up onto his head.

"So did you need something?" I blurted, not wanting to get caught practically drooling over his appearance.

"Nope. I thought maybe you might want to hang out today."

"You wanna hang out?" I asked skeptically. Brody didn't seem like the kind of guy who liked to "hang out."

"Figured you might not want to be alone."

"I've been alone for all of ten minutes." I scoffed. "My father—" I stopped midsentence, getting a very bad feeling I knew what this was really about.

I moved to cross my arms over my chest, but I couldn't because of the stupid sling. So I settled for a glare.

"What?" Brody asked warily.

"Is he paying you to be here?" I practically growled. It was totally something he would do. If he had his way, I'd have as many guards as the president, which was totally ridiculous.

He didn't have to confirm it with words because the look on his face said it all.

Fury and embarrassment warred inside me. This was totally not going to happen. I yanked the door back open and gestured to it. "Leave."

Brody stared at me levelly, a little bit of surprise flickering behind his eyes.

I blew out a breath, irritated he wasn't listening. "I'm not trying to air-condition the front porch," I snapped, hoping he would take the hint and get to walking.

Finally, he started moving, strolling oh so casually over to the door. I stiffened a little as he moved past me. I wished he hadn't been paid to be here. I wished he came because he wanted to.

Brody grabbed the edge of the door and swung it closed. "No," he said, turning to look at me, a challenge in his eyes.

"I don't want you here," I growled. I was so angry and so embarrassed that I felt a rush of tears behind my eyes.

Oh, hell no, I commanded myself. *You will not let this jerk-wad see you cry.* It was hard to hold off those tears. I was tired, I was hurt, and now I looked like a pathetic, helpless girl whose daddy paid people to be around her.

"Too bad."

"I will not be a *job* to you!" I burst out and then ran for the stairs. "Get out!" I flung the words over my shoulder as I went.

He caught me as I placed my foot on the bottom step, pulling me around and pushing me up against the wall. "This isn't a job to me," he growled, his eyes hard.

Looked like he didn't enjoy being bossed around either.

"How much did he offer you?" I spat.

"A hundred grand."

I gasped. My father was completely insane. For years, I humored his overprotective tendencies. Hell, I even understood them. But enough was enough. This was absolutely humiliating.

"Let go of me." I tried to pull away, but he moved in closer, pinning me with his rock-solid body.

"I turned it down."

It took a moment for his words to break through the angry cloud swarming my head. I paused and glanced up. "You what?"

"I don't want your father's money. This isn't a job to me."

I snorted. Brody made it perfectly clear from the beginning this whole situation was a job. "Yeah? Then what is it?"

"An excuse."

"An excuse…" I echoed.

"To spend time with you."

I snorted again. "You expect me to believe that you turned down one hundred thousand dollars because you *want* to spend time with me?"

He grinned lazily and the bottom dropped out of my belly. "Yep."

"I have a hole in my arm, not in my head."

His voice dropped and his mouth drew near. "Did you like my kisses?"

My brain knew what he was doing and Brody clearly knew the effect he had on me. He knew his manly charm, sexy tattoos, and hushed voice controlled me far better than anything else ever could. But even as I recognized his methods of distraction, I couldn't stop them from working.

His dark, bottomless eyes dropped to my lips. "Did you, Taylor?"

"You know I did." I was going for exasperated… All I managed was breathless.

He leaned in even closer. I could feel the heat off his skin, the breath off his lips. His eyes drooped closed even as I watched him, mesmerized by every single thing about him.

Just as our lips matched up, he lifted his chin ever so slightly, tilting his head up so the tips of our noses brushed together. Leaning just a little to the side, his bottom lip brushed over my top one, dragging upward, and our noses brushed together again. My limbs started shaking because just one brief touch wasn't enough.

Watching him still, I tilted up my own head, the back of my head sliding against the wall as I lifted, realigning our mouths and inviting him to take advantage.

Brody opened his eyes, spearing me with the molten chocolate of his irises. The heat I saw in his gaze was undeniable. The desire he exuded could only be real. His hand flattened out on the wall right beside my head and he shifted his stance, sliding one of his thighs between my legs.

And then he lifted.

That powerful thigh I was admiring in his jeans just moments ago slid upward, bringing me with it. My feet hovered over the floor as I straddled his thigh, the firmness of his muscle pressing right against my core. The sweet spot inside my panties began to throb heavily with the seductive pressure of my position against the wall.

And he kissed me.

Brody diminished the scant distance between us and sealed our lips together. I reacted eagerly, taking everything he would give me and letting it fill up my insides. His tongue swept inside my mouth and I groaned. I loved the width of his tongue. I loved the way it stroked like it intended to possess everything it touched.

I couldn't help but rock against his thigh, and when I moved, so did he, bringing it up a little bit more. A sensation of pleasure shot through me, and my inner muscles contracted, squeezing together, trying to milk every last bit of excitement from that movement. As soon as it faded, I rocked again, groaning into his mouth while my fingers found the waistband of his jeans and tried to yank him closer.

My body was demanding. It wanted more. It wanted to be brought to the very top of a mountain and then shoved off, plummeting me into the deep abyss of pleasure.

Brody broke the kiss and drew in a ragged breath. I could feel the way his abs contracted with every quick breath he took. I was wearing an oversized chambray shirt over a pair of leggings and I hadn't bothered to button it all the way to the top. Brody slid his palm into the opening at my neck and pulled away the fabric, exposing my collarbone and shoulder, scooping down and scraping his teeth across my flesh.

I tingled as the sharp edges scraped over my flesh and shuddered when he went back over the same spot with that wicked tongue of his. I tried to lean forward, to kiss any part of him I could reach, but he pinned me back, shaking his head, and dove into the side of my neck like he was some kind of starved vampire.

But he didn't bite me. He sucked at the flesh, drawing it into his mouth, and the tugging sensation made my thighs tighten around his leg.

My hand ripped away from the waistband of his jeans and I thrust it up beneath the hem of his shirt, drawing my nails across his washboard abs, traveling up so I could cup his pec in my palm. The second I brushed over his nipple, it tightened into a rock-hard pebble, and I grasped it between two fingers and pinched.

A hoarse sound ripped from his throat and he stopped kissing me, his head buried in my neck. I actually felt slight trembling throughout his limbs, and knowing he was just as turned on by me as I was him was a heady aphrodisiac.

Feeling a little bolder, I pinched his nipple again, twisting it slightly, and he shuddered. I rotated my hips over his thigh and made a little purring sound.

"Damn, Taylor," he groaned, pulling back to look down at me. "You make it really hard to stop."

I didn't ask him to stop. In fact, I wanted him to continue.

Brody slowly lowered his leg until my feet touched the floor. When he stepped back, I had to give more of my weight to the wall because without the support, I would have collapsed in a quivering puddle.

"Every time I kiss you," he rasped, brushing a finger across my cheek, "your skin turns a shade of pink."

"Curse of a redhead." I smiled.

"It's not a curse. It's damn cute."

I wrinkled my nose. I didn't want to be cute, not to him. I wanted to be sexy. I wanted to make him flustered with need. It was only fair because that's the effect he had on me.

"Are you hungry?" I asked, changing the subject. I didn't care to talk about my cuteness. And trying to make him leave again was useless. I wasn't completely positive that he really did just want to spend time with me, but I didn't want him to go.

"I'm always hungry."

"Come along, then," I called, trailing through the house and into the kitchen where the scent of cinnamon and vanilla drifted through the air.

I glanced at the untouched French toast bake on the counter and felt my stomach rumble since the first time I left the hospital. After pulling out a tub of butter from the fridge, I opened the cupboard to reach inside to grab a couple plates.

The muscles in my body protested when I stretched up to reach and a renewed sense of weariness washed over me. I didn't like feeling this way so I tried to ignore my feelings.

Brody came up behind me, invading my personal space, sandwiching me between the counter and his chest. I resisted the urge to sink back into him, the comfort of his body so enticing.

"What the hell are you doing?" he asked, brushing away my arm and reaching onto the top shelf with ease. "You shouldn't be moving around so much."

"I figured eating off plates would be better than our hands," I quipped. I mean really, like putting food on a plate was that taxing.

When he lowered his arm (plates in hand), he brushed against the side of my body and leaned in close to whisper in my ear. "I like a woman with a little bit of attitude."

I snatched the plates from his hand and spun, only he stayed where he was. My breasts brushed against his chest, and beneath my clothing, my nipples tightened. "It's getting cold," I said. The proximity of his body was like someone handing you a hot fudge sundae just dripping with sweetness and telling you not to eat it.

He smirked and stepped aside, letting me by. I shoved away from the counter and went to the granite-topped island where the French toast was cooling.

"You really shouldn't be in here cooking," he admonished again. I heard the concern in his voice so I decided to ignore his potent bossiness because it was clear he really did care about my wellbeing.

"I didn't make this," I told him, setting out the plates and picking up a knife to cut into the thick bread-and-egg mixture. "My Dad has a housekeeper that also does some cooking. She was here this morning, but I sent her home."

"Trying to get rid of your babysitter?"

"Yeah, and then you showed up." I glanced over my shoulder to mock scowl at him. The scowl didn't go very well though because I was completely distracted by the way he leaned his hip into the counter and casually flung out his leg. His arms were folded over his chest and the tattoos on his arms were in full view.

Did I mention I really, *really* liked the way he looked?

"I'm not so bad, am I?" He gave me a knowing smile.

I plopped a huge helping of the casserole on a plate, added a little butter, a drizzle of syrup, a fork, and handed it to him. I wasn't about to tell him just before he arrived I had wished I could see him.

He took the plate, scooped up a huge forkful, and shoved it in his mouth.

"You're going to choke," I admonished.

"You know mouth to mouth?" he asked around the food he was chewing.

I rolled my eyes and served myself a much more sensible piece. I sat down on one of the nearby stools and Brody came over to sit beside me. "What is this?" he asked, shoving yet another huge bite into his mouth. Then he growled. "It's good."

"It's pumpkin French toast bake. She makes it a lot. It is really good," I replied, taking a bite. The bread melted in my mouth and the sugary sweetness of the syrup slid over my tongue.

"Is she single?" he asked.

"I think so."

"Think she'd marry me?"

I snorted. "She's twice your age."

"I like a woman with experience," he quipped, shoving the last bite into his mouth.

I knew he was only teasing, but part of me felt a little disappointed. It was clear by the way he kissed and by the way he moved that Brody was very experienced. While I had dated, my experience was a lot less than his.

I pushed another bite into my mouth to avoid having to reply. He pushed off the stool and went to the coffeemaker sitting on the counter. "How do you work this thing?"

"Just push the start button. It should already be ready to brew."

A little beep filled the silence and then the fresh scent of brewing coffee filled the room. "So do you live here with your dad?" he asked as he helped himself to another huge piece of French toast.

"If he had his way I would," I answered, setting aside my fork. "But, no, I live a few miles away in a townhouse. My best friend lives there with me, but right now she's in Europe."

"So you're staying here."

"For now." Brody returned to the stool right beside me and I turned toward him. "He's very protective, to the point of frustration, but I can also understand."

"Is it just you and him?"

I nodded. "For the last two years. My mom passed away from breast cancer. Before she died, he wasn't as bad as he is now, but losing her was…" I paused and cleared my throat. Just thinking of her and the pain she went through before the disease finally claimed her life caused emotion to well up inside me. "It was really hard. Now I'm all he has left."

"Cancer sucks," Brody said, shoving another bite into his mouth.

I laughed. I was so used to hearing the obligatory, "I'm so sorry for your loss," that having him come right out and say what he was thinking was refreshing. "Yes, it does."

"I figure you take after your mom in the looks department?"

"Yes, I look a lot like her. Which I think is also another reason my father is so protective."

"Makes sense."

"What about you? Do your parents live around here?" I asked as he finished up his second plate of food.

"They live outside of Raleigh. I don't see them much."

"Do you have any brothers and sisters?"

"I have a brother, but I don't see him much either."

"Oh." I was very close to my father and mother before she died. I'd always wanted siblings, but by the time my parents thought of having more, my mother was diagnosed with breast cancer and having more children wasn't an option. She went into remission when I was ten, for several years, but then it came back. She fought it for a very long time, but eventually her body just couldn't fight anymore.

"With the kind of life I live, the kind of job I do, it's safer for my family not be around me so much," he explained, watching me.

"That sounds lonely." My heart ached for him. I knew he thought staying away from his family was only helping them, but what about him? He didn't have anyone.

"I'm hardly ever alone."

"But are you surrounded by people you actually like?"

"You need to eat more than two bites," he told me, ignoring my question. Brody picked up my fork and stabbed a bite of food on it to hold up to my mouth.

I parted my lips, allowing him to slip the food inside.

I didn't ask the question again because his lack of response was a very telling answer. Brody was lonely. He was just either too blind to see it or too stubborn to admit it.

15

Brody

Her hair was in two thick braids that fell over her shoulders. Her black pants were like a second skin and the loose, blue shirt buttoned up over her body couldn't disguise how sexy she was. She still seemed a little worn out, with light-purple smudges beneath her eyes, but even tired, she was beautiful.

I wasn't used to thinking of women as beautiful. Hot? Yes. Desirable? Of course. Likable? Sometimes. But never beautiful.

There wasn't much beauty in the world I lived in. Even physical beauty could be overshadowed by what lay just beneath the surface. Living in the ghetto, living deep undercover for years taught me that. Usually, if I did meet a woman who could be considered beautiful, she ruined it all by opening her mouth, getting into a bar fight, or ho-ing herself out to every guy she thought would give her a little bit more than what she already had.

The streets weren't kind to beauty. Beauty was easily corrupted. Beauty was easily tarnished.

Taylor was untarnished. Her beauty remained even after she opened her mouth. In fact, her beauty intensified. I might not like her father, but he did right by this girl. He shielded her, he took care of her, and he kept the rareness of her beauty intact. Sure, he was a little overprotective, but the more time I spent with Taylor, the more I understood.

Even guarded by money and a loving father hadn't kept her innocent. I was glad for that. I was too corrupt for innocence. True, I didn't know her very well, but I knew enough to see she had the kind of backbone a person only formed when adversity stepped in their path.

But never mind her backbone and beauty.

Kissing her made me crazy.

So crazy that it was practically all I could think about. I was like an addict who only wanted their next fix. Just the mere thought of her lips, of her full bottom lip, turned my cock to granite.

I wasn't lying when I said her father's request was just an excuse. An excuse to be near her, to get in her. And I wanted in her. I wanted to bury myself so deep in her body that I couldn't tell where I ended and she began.

But I couldn't.

Not yet anyway. I had to wait until she was sure I wasn't here because her father paid me to be.

So I followed her into the kitchen to eat some awesome-ass French toast. But her laugh got to me. Her closeness got to me. And the way she seemed to identify what I was feeling when I myself had no idea got to me.

That sounds lonely.

Yeah, maybe I was. Or maybe I was just tired of trying to be two different people. Maybe I didn't know who I was at all. I kinda felt homesick… only I had no home to go to.

"Hey you wanna get out of here?" I asked as I fed her yet another bite of breakfast. I might not be able to go home, but I could go to the last place I felt relaxed.

"Where?" she asked, chewing thoughtfully. Just the movement of her lips as she ate was enough to make me contemplate bending her over the stool she was sitting on and taking her.

"Fishing," I said, my voice husky.

I abandoned her fork and plate to get up and rummage through one of the hundreds of cabinets (seriously, what man needed this many cabinets?) for a coffee mug.

"You want to go fishing?"

I grunted as I opened yet another door to look.

"They're over here," she said from close by. Taylor opened a cabinet and reached in to pull out a white mug. When I reached out to take it, she yanked it back, stuffing it back into the cabinet.

"Hey…"

She grinned over her shoulder and then turned back. "I need up," she said, pointing to the highest shelf in the cupboard.

I could have moved her aside and reached for whatever it was she wanted.

I didn't do that.

Instead, I wrapped my hands around her waist, loving the supple feeling of her body under my hands. The sides of her waist dipped in like it was made just for my hands. "Up you go," I said, easily lifting her and wrapping an arm around her hips to anchor her against me as she reached for whatever she wanted.

Her little giggle made my stomach flip.

After several seconds, she patted me on the arm. "Got it."

Careful of her injured arm, I let her slide down the front of my body. When her ass hit my crotch, my hips moved without thought and thrust toward her, bringing my throbbing length right up against her.

The travel mugs she was holding fell onto the counter, and she melted back against me. I reached around her front and filled my hand with her breast, wishing her bulky shirt wasn't in my way. She made a little sound of appreciation and I squeezed, kneading the mound with firm, confident strokes.

Taylor's arm came up to snake around my neck. Her fingers slid up the back into my hairline, making little chills of need race all way into my toes. Keeping her hand around the back of my neck, she slowly pivoted around, her body brushing mine as she turned and looked up at me with darkened emerald eyes.

Damn, I fucking loved seeing that look on her face.

Like I was her entire world.

Her hand pulled me down so our lips could meet, could caress each other in a slow, lazy kiss. There was no tongue involved this time, but it didn't matter.

Her nails raked down the side of my neck and over my chest, traveling down until it fell completely away. I pulled back, actually feeling fuzzy headed.

No girl ever made me feel dazed before.

"You pour us some coffee to go, and I'll get the hot dogs."

My brain was still operating a few batteries short. "Hot dogs?" I asked.

She gave me a half smile. "For the fish."

Oh, yeah. We were going fishing. Who the hell came up with that idea? Sex was a much better way to pass the time.

"Brody?" The tentative way she said my name, almost like asking a question, drew me out of my dirty (yet satisfying) thoughts.

"Yeah?"

"Did you change your mind?"

"What would you say if I did?" I asked, lifting an eyebrow. I stepped toward her, reaching around to grab her ass. "What would you say if I told you I'd rather stay in?"

Her body swayed toward me and her chin tipped back. "I'd ask you what you would rather do."

That was not the answer I was hoping to get. She was supposed to say she didn't want to stay in. She was supposed to act like what I was proposing was dirty and offensive.

I liked dirty and offensive.

She wasn't supposed to as well.

It made me want her even more.

I growled and gave her ass cheek another squeeze and then pushed back to go make the coffee. I was making damn coffee when I could be ripping off her clothes.

I was out of my damn mind.

A short while later, we were sitting in my old Ford, heading down I-40 toward Lake Crabtree. It was a hot day, but rather than turn on the AC, we rolled down the windows. At first I thought she might worry about her hair or something equally girly, but she didn't. Instead, she laughed and stuck her hand out the window, allowing her fingers to play in the passing wind.

Wisps of cinnamon hair escaped the playful braids over her shoulders and caught in the breeze, tugging all around her head. Almost immediately after climbing into the cab of the truck, she discarded her shoes and propped her bare feet up on the dashboard. Her feet were dainty and her toes were painted pink.

For a woman I knew came from money, who had the best offered to her from an early age, she seemed comfortable in my old beat-up truck with fishing poles rattling around in the back. Country music came through the radio and neither of us spoke, but sometimes she would sing along in an off-key, enthusiastic voice.

About twenty minutes after leaving her house, we turned into Lake Crabtree County Park. Sweeping views of the five-hundred-and-twenty-acre lake sparkling in the sun was a welcome sight. After we parked and I rented a small rowboat, we threw two fishing poles, a tackle box, and the hot dogs onto the wooden floor.

I grabbed an orange life jacket and held it out. "In you go."

"I know how to swim."

"Humor me."

She stared at me mutinously for long moments, but then she relented with a sigh and held out her good arm. "You want me to take off this sling?"

"Nope," I said and fastened the jacket around her, essentially leaving her one-armed.

"How am I supposed to fish?" she complained.

"I'll help you." Before she could protest any more, I lifted her into the boat and waited for her to take a seat.

"Don't you want help pushing it out into the water?"

I held up my arm, flexing my bicep. It was big and manly. "You see these guns? I don't need help."

"Bossy and full of yourself," she muttered.

A few moments later, we were floating in the gentle waves of the lake. I began to row us out farther into the water, where we could find a really good spot to fish.

"This looks like a good place," she said a little bit later, gazing out across the water to the other side where there was nothing but trees growing close together.

I stuck the oar I was holding straight down into the water, giving the spot a depth test.

"What are you doing?" she asked.

"There are some shallow spots in this lake that are only three feet deep." The oar hit the bottom of the lake floor as if to prove my point. "Let's go out a little farther away from this spot for better fishing."

"It's really pretty here," she said, once again staring out over the expansive view. "We used to come here when I was a little girl. My mom would bring a picnic."

"I used to come out here too. My grandfather always brought me and my brother to fish."

Off behind us, the lake stretched until there was nothing but a line of trees, almost creating a border around the water. To the right, there was a single-lane paved road that wound around the side. It was the same road we traveled down to get to the boat rental place.

For those that didn't want to fish from a boat, there was a fishing pier and platform that we could see perfectly from out here in the water.

"There aren't many people here today," she said, following my stare toward the pier.

"It's a workday and its afternoon. Most of the serious fisherman would come early in the morning." The only people on the pier were a man and young boy who were casting out a fishing line with a brightly colored bobber attached to the line.

When we drove in, we saw several groups of people in the picnic areas and there was also some sailboats and kayaks in the distance.

"So you work at the bank?" I asked as I baited our two fishing lines with hot dog pieces.

She nodded, pushing the loose strands of hair away from her face. "Yes, my father wants me to someday take over."

"But you don't want to?"

"Actually, I do," she said, taking the pole I offered. I watched as she deftly pressed the button on the reel and successfully cast out the line

"Nice," I told her, admiring her sure movements.

She gave me a grin before continuing to answer my question. "I actually have a degree in accounting. I've always liked math. Numbers make sense to me."

"Then what were you doing at the teller counter?"

"My father thinks a successful CEO of any corporation—including his bank—knows all aspects of the business. So after I graduated college, I came to work at the bank, and I have been spending time in each position, learning the inner workings of the entire business."

As much as I hated to admit it, I admired her father. Yes, he was powerful and successful, but it was because he worked for it, and he was making sure she did as well.

"Can I ask you something?" she asked.

"Anything."

"What's it like being an undercover cop?"

"Sometimes it's confusing," I admitted, the confession ripping out of me from deep inside.

"Confusing how?"

"Sometimes I forget what side I'm on."

She jumped in her seat, leaping back a little and giving a small squeal. For a second, I thought I made a mistake, being so nakedly honest. I probably scared her; she probably thought she was sitting here with a bad guy masquerading as a good one.

Maybe she was.

"I got a bite!" she exclaimed, tugging back on the rod and turning excited eyes on me. She tugged the rod again and lost her balance, slipping backward over the little seat she was perched upon. I surged forward, rocking the boat to steady her.

"I think you might need some help." I said into her ear. "Might be tough to reel in a fish with only one hand."

Taylor leaned back into me, her back completely melding into my chest as I took the rod out of her hand. She seemed content to allow me to do all the work, pulling in the fish while she sat in the circle of my body.

I began turning the little handle, slowly towing in the fish. "The key to not losing the fish is to go nice and slow," I murmured right against her ear.

A little shiver jerked her body and I smiled, liking the effect I had on her.

I adjusted my hands so that my hold on the rod was a little tighter – really I just wanted to hold her closer. "You have to let the water caress the fish as you reel it in, so that when it comes up out of the water its relaxed."

"Mmm-Hmm," she replied.

The fish was almost out of the water when I stopped turning and dipped down to press my lips against her cheek. Damn, she smelled so good.

On the end of the line the fish started to struggle so I pulled away from her and brought him up.

She shrieked when it appeared from the water, dripping and flopping around. "It's a big one!"

"Yep, it's a beauty."

I brought it over the side of the boat as it continued to flop around.

"It's pretty," she said, admiring her catch.

She made no move at all to leave my arms. In fact, she stayed leaning against me, resting her head against my chest. The fish flopped again and smacked into her ankle. She shrieked and pulled her leg away, shrinking against me.

"Are you telling me you're afraid to touch it?"

"It's slimy!"

Unbelievable. There was that girly side coming out again. "I take it you aren't going to be the one to throw it back?"

"I'll leave that honor to you."

I scooped up the fish, gently pulled the hook out of its lip, and then dropped it over the side of the boat and back into the water.

"A girl who likes to fish but refuses to actually touch one," I muttered.

She giggled and watched the fish jump back into the water. I didn't bother re-baiting her hook. I liked sharing better. So I handed her my rod, which was lying abandoned off to the side. "Here, hold this," I said as I made myself more comfortable, spreading my thighs out behind her so she could settle more firmly against me.

After I took the rod back, I was contemplating recasting it when two black SUVs came around the curve in the road, following alongside the lakeshore. It wasn't anything unusual, but the hairs on the back of my neck stood up anyway.

I stared at the vehicles, unable to see behind the windshield because of the glare on the glass from the sun. My body stiffened as a feeling of foreboding came over me.

"Brody?" Taylor asked, sensing the change in my demeanor.

I sat the fishing rod down inside the boat as the SUVs swerved to the side of the road and stopped at the bank, directly across from where the boat floated.

"Get down, Taylor," I ordered, my voice urgent and low.

"Wh-what?" she said, her head swinging around to look at the men who were getting out of the cars.

One of them raised a pistol and pointed it right at me.

I surged to my feet, pushing her down into the bottom of the boat, and stood over her, turning toward the men.

"Brody," she called, and I hated the fear in her voice.

"Don't get up," I said and reached behind me into the waistband of my jeans for the .45 caliber I was carrying.

But their guns were already out.

"Fucking pig!" one of them yelled, and bullets started flying.

The first couple shots slammed into the water, making innocent splashing sounds, and then the third and fourth bullet hit the side of the boat. One of them plowed straight through the side, and water started seeping into the bottom of the vessel.

Taylor screamed.

Goddamn, we were sitting ducks out here in the center of the water with no protection at all.

I fired back and the men dove behind the SUVs, but I wasn't stupid enough to think those couple bullets would chase them away. Even as I thought it, one of the guys, wearing baggy jeans and a baseball hat pulled low, rose up from behind the hood to take aim at me once more.

I squeezed off a shot. My aim was true and the windshield he was standing by shattered instantly. He yelled a few curses and dove back down, taking cover from the raining glass.

I was a good shot, but there were three of them and only one of me. And they had cover, where I did not.

I didn't have any choice. It was a bullet or the water.

Just as the guys took aim again, I knocked the boat over, pitching us into the dark, cool lake.

16

Taylor

The water wasn't necessarily freezing cold, but it was a shock against my sun-heated skin. Everything happened so fast I barely had time to register what was going on, and then the all-too-familiar sounds of gunshots radiated through the air and literally paralyzed my limbs with fear.

Before I could do little more than scream, the boat was rocking violently and then Brody was flinging himself over me and launching into the water. But he didn't leave me alone. He turned the boat as he went so I was dumped right into the current.

The force of the movement pushed my body beneath the surface even as my arms and legs struggled to swim. I only had use of one arm because the life jacket and sling pinned the other one to my side.

My clothes were saturated instantly, the cool water soaking into my entire body. I blinked my eyes, too shocked to close them, and all I could see was the color brown. Dark, dirty water claimed me, and I blinked, trying to see anything else.

[159]

Panic seized my chest, robbing it of breath and creating this panicked explosive feeling in my lungs. Before I could start to worry I would drown, the lifejacket Brody insisted I wear did its job and pulled my body to the surface.

I gasped when my head cleared the water and used my only available arm to tread water. "Brody!" I screamed, blinking the water out of my eyes and searching for him.

More bullets rained through the air and cut through the water like a hot knife through butter. I shrieked and looked at the three men on shore who were firing at us openly, not even trying to hide the fact they were trying to commit murder.

I looked around, frantic for help. The man and young boy up on the pier were watching the unfolding scene. "Call 9-1-1!" I screamed as loud as I could.

Another bullet hit the water right beside me, and I dove away.

But I didn't go under. The jacket kept me afloat, and for once I wished it didn't work so well. I made a better target when those people with the guns could see me.

Something clamped around my ankle and I screamed, jerking away, trying to swim frantically and failing miserably. One-armed swimming was not something I excelled at.

Whatever was down there refused to let go, and then I was forced roughly beneath the surface. The life jacket fought against the weight, trying to tug me back up, but it was no use. Whatever had a hold of me was no match for the flotation device.

I felt my bandaged arm rub against the inside of the jacket and I winced because it hurt.

I was pulled farther down, my arm waving back and forth as I fought. Whatever it was towed me forward and then let go. I surfaced once more with a deep gasp; my lungs were burning from lack of oxygen.

I blinked the water out of my eyes and tried to locate the shooters, but all I saw was darkness.

I spun around, trying to figure out what was going on and where the sun went when an arm wrapped around my waist and another head broke the surface.

"Easy," Brody said, his voice a mere whisper.

I sobbed his name, not because I was scared, but because I was so relieved to see him. I flung my arm around his neck and latched onto him, like a sock with a bad case of static cling.

His arm closed around me and we both slid under the water just a little more from lack of paddling. "Tread the water," he said, releasing me. "We need to stay under the boat. It's the only protection we have."

Of course! I should have realized. Brody grabbed me from beneath the water and towed me under the capsized boat. It shielded us from criminal eyes and held a small pocket of air to allow us to breathe.

"Are you shot?" Brody asked, his voice hushed and insistent.

"No. Are you?"

"No."

"What's happening?" I asked. "Who are those guys?"

"Snake's been a busy guy," Brody murmured, lifting his gun out of the water and shaking it, trying to drain out all the moisture. "Seems he's ratted my identity out to everyone in the organization."

"You mean those are gang members who know you're a cop and want to kill you for it?"

"Did you hear them call me a pig?" Brody asked, trying to tread water and keep the gun from getting any wetter.

"It all happened so fast," I said, pushing heavy, wet strands of hair out of my face.

"Try to keep that arm still, okay?"

I nodded.

Another bullet hit the water and I could hear the guys talking amongst themselves on shore.

"Will they go away?" I whispered.

Even with the lack of light, I could see Brody grimace. "Remember that shallow area we passed on the way out here?" he asked, choosing not to answer my question.

"Yes."

"We're going to swim in that direction so it gives us some footing. We're going to tire out quickly if we have to keep treading."

"Okay."

"Stay with me, stay under this boat, and don't make any sudden movements or loud noises. We want it to look like the boat could just be drifting."

"Won't they know when we don't surface that we're under here?" I worried.

"Maybe," he allowed. "But if they can't see us, it will be harder to shoot us."

Another bullet struck the side of the boat, knocking a small, round hole in the wood. I jumped back, bumping into the very end.

Brody swore. "This wouldn't be happening right now if they'd managed to haul in Snake."

I bit my lower lip as cold seeped into my skin and the water made my clothes feel heavy. One of the flats I was wearing had already fallen off and was carried off by the current.

It was a shame. I really liked these shoes.

The bullet wound in my arm ached, and I worried about the stitches and bandages. I wasn't supposed to get that area of my arm wet. It was supposed to remain covered and dry for several more days.

"Come here," he said, reaching for me, towing me closer and anchoring me at his side. I couldn't help but notice the way he placed himself in front of me so he was stationed between my body and the side the men were shooting from.

We began moving together, slowly making our way toward where I hoped was a shallow area. My arm was burning and trembling slightly from the work of propelling my body through the water. Suddenly, I was extremely grateful that Brody strapped this life jacket on me, because without it, I would really be struggling.

I could hear his labored breathing in the tiny enclosed space. The air around our heads actually was uncomfortably warm, while the rest of me shivered with cold. I squinted through the darkness to make out his concentrated features as he pushed through the water, holding his gun above the surface, swimming and trying to tow the boat along as well.

I wished my arm wasn't rendered useless in this stupid sling. I tried to tug it free, figuring I would rather tear the stitches than drown, but the added confinement of the jacket made the task almost impossible.

More gunfire erupted and I heard the men at the bank watching for us, waiting for us to surface. They were debating on whether or not one of use was hit or if perhaps both of us drowned.

I can't say that listening to people plot my death was something I ever wanted to experience again.

"They're dead," one of the guys said. "Let's get the hell out of here."

"I'm not leaving 'til I know for sure. Snake wants confirmation."

"Fucking Snake," Brody spat. "I'm going to bring that asshole in myself."

I started to speak, but the words died in my throat because I needed the air to breathe. I felt like we'd been swimming for hours. Yeah, in reality it was only minutes, but my arm burned and begged for a break.

I kicked my legs a little harder to give my arm a rest, trying to push away the panic that was building inside me from being beneath this boat. It was beginning to feel entirely too claustrophobic.

I kicked out again and my toe hit something solid. I made a sound and yanked my foot away, my big toe throbbing like it had been stubbed.

"We found it," Brody said from right beside me. "Put your feet down to stand but don't stand up all the way."

I breathed a sigh of relief and stood in a crouch, my arm practically collapsing at my side. Brody turned to me. "Stay under here. If something happens to me, stay under this boat and wait for help."

Ice formed in my belly. He made it sound like he was leaving. "What are you doing?"

"I'm going to the surface and I'm going to shoot me some motherfuckers."

Oh my. His language was very bad. But damned if it didn't turn me on. *Now is not the time to be turned on,* I told myself. Brody started to move away, and I grabbed him.

"Wait! Stay here."

"I'm not staying here, Tay. I'm not the kind of guy who sits and waits. I'm the kind of guy who fights back."

"But you could get hurt." I felt a lump of grief rise up in my throat, making it hard to breathe and swallow.

"I'm not going to get hurt." He pressed a quick kiss to my lips and pulled away, causing water to lap against my chest.

And then he took a deep breath and went underwater, completely disappearing from sight. Barely several seconds later, I heard him break the surface and take a breath. I knew he was just on the other side of the boat, but it felt like he was miles away.

The faint sound of sirens in the distance was music to my ears. I whispered a silent thanks to the man who heard me cry for help and dialed 9-1-1.

Help was on the way.

The boat dipped a little, sinking down, and forced me farther into the water, up to my chin. A light tapping sound overhead made me look up, but of course I saw nothing. I knew it was Brody, but I had no idea what he was doing.

Surely he wouldn't climb up on top of the boat, giving those men an easy target.

"Look!" someone yelled. "There he is!"

What the hell was he thinking climbing on top of the boat?!

Before I could call out and tell him what a damn idiot he was being, the sound of gunfire filled the air.

17

Brody

I was pissed.

Actually, pissed was an understatement.

I felt like killing someone. And since I was an officer of the law, my life was being threatened, and so was the safety of the public, I had every right to shoot back.

So shoot the fuck back was what I was gonna do.

I might not have a home, per se, because the last few years of my life were spent in a rented, undercover, ugly-ass house with a granny-pink bathroom, but this lake was a place I'd been visiting since childhood. It was familiar, and it was as close to home as I had right now.

That meant these douche bags had come up in my house, shooting.

I knew Taylor was scared and wanted me to stick close by her side, but doing that wouldn't help our situation. So I left her beneath our pathetic excuse for a boat and came up to the surface. I was going to use the bottom of the boat as a shooting deck.

I knew I wouldn't get all three of them, but I might be able to bring down one or two. And once I did, I was going to make him talk.

I levered myself up and leaned against the side of the boat, letting my forearms rest on the top as I took aim with my .45 at the guys who were frantically watching the surface of the water for my body to start floating.

Just as I lined up my shot, one of the guys saw me and they all drew their weapons.

The first shot I fired hit one of the guys in the shoulder; the bullet slammed into him and sent him spiraling backward until his ass hit the dirt. One of his buddies looked down to help him, and I fired off another shot, catching him in the calf.

It was sick, but I enjoyed watching the bullet pummel his flesh as drops of red burst outward and speckled his skin. A couple shots came in my direction, one of them close enough that I felt the heat from the metal as it whizzed by my head.

I shot a couple more, causing the two guys who weren't lying on the ground bleeding to scatter backward.

The magazine in this gun only had about fifteen bullets in it, and I wasn't sure how many I already fired off. Five? Six? I didn't know, but I knew I only had so long to run these guys off.

The sound of sirens drew closer and I knew it would work to my advantage. The kid with the bleeding calf dragged himself over to the passenger side of the nearest SUV and scrambled inside. I shot the ground where he was standing to make him rush.

The remaining uninjured guy fired off a shot at me and I leapt back as the bullet grazed the top of the boat.

Taylor made a sound of distress, and my back teeth slammed together. It pissed me off she was in danger again.

The guy in the car was yelling for the other one to hurry, but he was slowed down by the fact he was trying to drag his bleeding, whining friend along with him. I shot at the ground again, scattering a little bit of earth up into his face. He dropped his buddy and looked up. I shot again, this time catching him in the hand gripping his gun.

He yelled and dropped the weapon. He didn't even glance back at his buddy this time. He just jumped in the SUV and drove off, leaving his "friend" to look out for himself.

Not only was he a killer, but he was dishonorable as well. It just went to show how desperate Snake was to get rid of me because he sent a loser like that to finish me off.

As soon as the dust flew up behind the getaway car, I shoved the gun in the back of my water-logged jeans and dove off the top of the boat. As I swam quickly toward shore, I felt the stitches in my side rip open, the sting of an open wound an unwelcome guest to this party.

By the time I made it to the bank, the abandoned crewmember had staggered to his feet, clutching the shoulder that hung unevenly from his body as it gushed copious amounts of blood. I hadn't really meant to hit an artery, but I wasn't sorry about it either.

I gave the guy ten minutes if he didn't get medical attention.

Ten minutes remained of his life, but I only needed about three.

I stalked the short distance from the bank and plowed into him. He stumbled and would have fallen, but I grabbed him by the front of his shirt and yanked. This time, he would have fallen forward, but my fist stopped him.

I plowed it into his jaw, enjoying the burst of energy I felt move through my body when my fist rammed his flesh.

He made a groaning sound and fell onto his back, rocking a little, trying to stop the pain. I leaned over him, grabbing his blood-soaked shirt once again. "Where's Snake?" I demanded.

He coughed, little drops of blood scattering over his face.

"Where. Is. Snake?" I ground out again.

"I don't know." He lied.

I shoved my thumb into the bullet wound. He screamed. The squishy flesh felt spongy beneath my finger and blood oozed anew.

"Tell me!" I roared, pulling back my fist to hit him again.

I wasn't above torture. These were criminals. Known druggies, killers, and thieves. They were tough, but I knew how to make them talk because I learned from them.

His lip split when I punched him, and his head snapped to the side.

"Downtown Raleigh," he said, coughing and spewing more blood.

"Where?" I gave my fist a rest and just glared down at him.

"25th street. Apartment A."

I yanked him up a little farther so I could stare directly in his face. "You better not be lying."

He grinned; his teeth were outlined in red. "We both know I'm dead either way. Might as well take down the guy who sent me here."

"Enjoy hell," I spat and tossed him onto the pavement as two patrol cars ripped around the corner with their lights flashing.

"See you there," he whispered as I turned away.

His final words would likely haunt me. Not because they were threatening, but because they were true.

The cop cars skidded to a stop and they both flung their doors open and crouched behind them, raising their guns at me.

"I'm officer Brody West," I called, lifting my hands. "Two of the perps took off that way in a black SUV. One of the passengers is shot."

One of the officers jumped back in his car and drove off in the direction I pointed.

The other one lowered his gun and walked cautiously around the hood of his car. "What the hell is going on, West?" he said, and I recognized him as one of the officers who was part of the bust at the old gas station the other night.

"My cover is blown. Thanks to Snake, I just became the most wanted cop within the organization."

Officer Newman shook his head and bent down to check the pulse of the man lying on the ground. "He's dead."

"I shot him after he opened fired on me and my girl." Thoughts of Taylor had me dismissing the case and spinning toward the water where I left the boat.

Fear spiked in my veins as I imagined the worst: that she got hit again and was bleeding out or drowning while I was over here beating a guy for the last moments of his life.

What the hell kind of man was I?

But Taylor wasn't dead.

She wasn't floating in the water or bleeding out.

But she wasn't hiding under the boat anymore either. Instead, she stood in front of it, soaking wet and pale, looking toward me and the officer with a drawn look on her face.

I knew then she saw what I had done.

She saw the way I got the information I needed.

And she didn't like it.

Suddenly, I felt like some adolescent kid who brought home four D's and an F on my report card and I was standing there silently awaiting judgment by my mother.

Fuck that.

I was a grown-ass man and sometimes I had to do things most people would think were shitty. But I did them because they needed to be done. Because sometimes getting answers required getting my hands dirty.

At least she had the luxury to pass judgment on me. She wouldn't if I didn't act the way I did.

"You got this?" I asked Officer Newman, motioning to the body with my chin.

"Yeah."

I went back into the lake, swimming out to where Taylor stood barely moving as she watched me draw closer.

When my feet hit the bank of the shallow section, I stood up, looking down into her jade eyes. "Are you hurt?"

"No."

"How's the arm?"

"Wet."

I felt my lips twitch but forced them not to smile.

"Come on." I offered her my hand. "We can't row the boat back, but I'll help you to shore."

She gazed down at my hand stretched out between us and then looked up. She recognized the test I was giving her. She knew her reaction to my offer would likely tell me everything I needed to know.

Did I still have a chance with her?

Or…

Would watching me shoot a man, then beat him make her shrink away from my touch?

She looked at my hand for long moments before reaching up and pushing it aside. I won't lie; something inside me sank a little. Her rejection (even though suspected) stung like hell.

Before I could turn away, she moved, not away, but closer. Instead of taking my offered hand, she leaned up and wrapped her arm around my middle and pressed in close against my chest. It took me a minute to react, a minute for my brain to catch up to what my body was already feeling. I brought up my arms; they kind of hovered behind her. I was almost afraid to hug her, to hold her close. What if she changed her mind?

"I'm sorry you had to do that," she said, her voice muffled against my wet T-shirt.

"You saw?" I asked, wanting to make certain she saw it all.

"Yes, I saw."

I lowered my arms back to my sides. "It isn't the first time I've done something like that. I've done worse." My heart was thumping slowly in my chest, almost like it was hesitating the same way my arms had.

[172]

I hadn't realized how important her opinion of me had become in such a short amount of time. I realized I wanted to be worthy of her. I wanted her to see past the man I was paid to be, to somehow look inside me and see the man I'd forgotten.

"I know," she whispered. "It's okay."

My heart stuttered. "What?"

Her head tipped back. "I don't care, Brody. I know that's not who you are."

I didn't hesitate a second time. I wrapped my arms around her, holding her close. "It's part of me." I cautioned, not knowing why I bothered. I shouldn't try to push her away, not now, not after something inside me already claimed her. Whatever part was holding me back was broken and now lay shattered at my feet.

She pulled back. "You're a lot like an uncut diamond."

Was this one of those moments when her complete girliness was going to come out? Why the hell was she talking about diamonds?

"An uncut diamond has a rough exterior and maybe even a couple flaws, but underneath are brilliant qualities."

"You think I'm brilliant?" I asked, feeling a grin split my face.

"I might not go that far." She scoffed.

A weight I didn't even know I bore lifted off me, and for the first time in a long time, I felt like maybe I wasn't as lost to myself as I thought.

It was a good feeling.

"Does this mean you believe you're more than a job to me?" I asked, stepping up close and invading her personal space. I liked invading her space. I wanted to get *all up* in her space.

"I believe you."

It was like someone gave my dick a green light because the minute the words left her mouth, blood began flowing down into my pants, like an insane adrenaline rush that only happened in my lower body.

Another patrol car and an ambulance pulled up to the scene, and I was reminded that this wasn't a good time for my *other* brain to take control. I ducked down in the water and offered Taylor my back. "Come on. I'll do the swimming."

Once her arm and legs were fastened around me, I swam the short distance to shore, where everyone was waiting to take our statements.

The first thing I did was set Taylor down in the back of the ambulance and tell them to check her stitches. "Don't give them a hard time this go around, 'kay?" I told her after draping a blanket around her body. Then I pressed a kiss to her damp hairline and left her in the capable hands of the EMTs.

Officer Newman was standing beside the body, along with two other officers I knew from the RPD. "Before he died, he told me where Snake was hiding."

They all looked up, interested.

"I want a patrol car out there now to pick up his weasely ass before word of what happened here gets to him." That reminded me of the two men who ran off before the police arrived.

"What about the runaway black SUV?" I asked.

"All in custody," Newman answered.

I nodded. Then we still had time to get to Snake before someone else did. He might have been able to get away and hide in practically plain sight for the last couple days, but he made a mistake.

He came after me… after Taylor.

"Let's go. We need to go make the arrest."

"Uh, West?" said the officer beside Newman, looking at me.

"What?"

"You might wanna go get looked at by a medic." He pointed to my side where the torn stitches were bleeding anew and a red stain was spreading across my drenched shirt.

I sighed. I was getting sick of bleeding.

"Let us handle the arrest," Newman said, slapping me on the back. "You have enough to deal with."

Refusal was on the tip of my tongue. I wanted to be there to see the look on Snake's face when they slapped some cuffs on his wrists. I wanted the satisfaction of being there when he went down.

I glanced over my shoulder at Taylor, who was huddled in the back of the ambulance, frowning at the EMT who was cutting away the drenched bandages on her wound. If I left now, then no one would be here with her but strangers.

I couldn't leave her here alone.

"Yeah, okay." I relented. "I should probably get this sewn back up." I pointed to my side. "Some dry clothes might be nice too."

Newman nodded briskly and then looked at the man next to him. "Let's go make the arrest."

The pair started off toward a cruiser, and I called out behind them. "Call me the minute he's in custody."

Newman waved and drove away.

I felt Taylor's stare and turned, our eyes connecting from several yards away. A possessive feeling unfolded inside me and an urgent need clawed its way to the surface. Usually, I claimed a woman with nothing but my body—with nothing but my dick. But this was wholly different. I hadn't even had her in that way yet, but she was already mine.

And as soon as this mess was cleaned up here, I was going to have her completely.

18

Taylor

It was not quite dinnertime when Brody finally pulled his truck into the driveway of my dad's house. After everything that happened, the hour felt like it should be much later.

Thankfully, neither one of us needed to make another trip to the hospital. My stitches were looked at, the area around them was cleaned, dried, and then a new bandage was applied. They even gave me a new sling, which I refused to put on until I got out of these annoyingly wet and grimy clothes.

Brody required a couple new stitches, which he insisted they do right there instead of him going to the hospital. Since his shirt was also drenched with water, he opted not to wear it home (and just ruin the new dressing over his stitches), so I had been constantly trying (and failing) not to stare at his hard body and chiseled muscles.

I found myself daydreaming the entire ride home about using my tongue to trace along the tattooed path of the vine that wound its way down his arm.

My father wasn't home yet and I didn't expect him until very late. Since the robbery, he and all the executives had been working practically around the clock, putting out fires and dealing with angry members. Thankfully, word hadn't gotten out about what happened today, so I opted not to tell him just yet, but to wait until things calmed down. There was really no use in worrying him anyway. He already had enough to worry about.

And truthfully…

I knew if I told him, he would come home. I didn't want him to come home. I wanted to be alone with Brody.

The stark possessiveness and want in his eyes made my toes curl against the floorboard of the truck and my teeth chew the inside of my lip with mouth-watering anticipation. My God, the thought of his rippling muscles and sleek tattoos sliding over my pale and boring body was enough to stop the heart in my chest.

The inside of the house was quiet and felt cold. It wasn't that the AC was turned especially low; it was more because I was still slightly chilled from our impromptu dunk in the lake. Goose bumps raced over my skin as we stepped into the house and locked up the door behind us.

"I need to get out of these clothes," I said, my eyes straying down to the black duffle bag in Brody's hand.

I looked away and pressed a hand between my breasts, trying to rub away the ache that formed there. When I suggested we stop at his place to get him a change of clothes, he told me he didn't have a place of his own.

Since closing the case he had been working on for years, he was literally living out of a suitcase. The

[178]

thought of him spending so much time alone in hotel room after hotel room and keeping all his possessions in the bed of his truck hurt me. I knew the reasons he pushed away his family, but now that the case was over, why didn't he go see them? Surely his mother would open up her home to him.

Of course, judging from the way he expected me to act after I watched him force Snake's location out of that man, he seemed to think he didn't deserve to be welcomed by his family.

"Come on," I said, leading the way up the staircase and down to the end of the hall where I pushed open a white door and stepped into my room. It was spacious, with a queen-sized bed taking up the center of the room. The headboard was tufted cream fabric that reached nearly to the ceiling, and all the bedding was monochromatic in shades of white. At the foot of the bed there was a long, velvet-covered bench in an apple-green color. The floors were carpeted with a light neutral shade, and I kicked off my one remaining shoe and let my toes sink into the plush softness. The far wall had three large windows side by side, with white wooden blinds, which were still closed, and cream-colored drapes with large apple-green polka dots covering the fabric. I thought it added a touch of whimsy into an otherwise elegant and calming room.

Aside from the bed, there was a tall console table that held a few picture frames and a vase of white flowers. Above it hung a flat-screen TV. Off to the left was the entrance for the attached bath, which was also done up in very light neutral shades.

"Nice," Brody said, closing the door behind him and setting his duffle on the bench at the end of the bed.

"It's bigger than my room at my apartment." I smiled. I laid the sling on the end of the bed so I could put it on later, once I was dry.

"You can change out here. My clothes are in the closet just off the bathroom."

He fastened his gaze on me and prowled across the room, abandoning his bag, intent on his prey.

His prey = me.

"You need some help?" he asked, stopping in front of me and fingering the buttons holding my shirt together.

I nodded, unable to actually form a word.

Slowly, his large hands undid each small button, one by one. With every one he freed, my shirt opened just a little bit more. When he got to the buttons at my waist, he allowed his knuckles to brush against my abdominals, and I sucked in a breath.

Once all the buttons were free, he took both his hands and slid them into the neck of the button-up, slipping easily right beneath the collar. He drew his hands over my shoulders and down to the center of my back, gently pulling away the shirt, gradually exposing more and more of my skin.

My injured arm wasn't in the sleeve of my shirt. I hadn't bothered to fit it back in after changing my bandages. So that side completely fell away, and the shirt was left to dangle behind me, just beneath my shoulder. Brody dragged his hands down the back of my arms (avoiding my injury) and tossed the shirt onto the floor.

My nipples were so tight beneath my bra they actually hurt, and even though I was wearing a semi-padded undergarment, my nipples showed through like the sun on a cloudless day.

Brody bent his head, his lips fastened on the top of my shoulder, and he trailed moist kisses from the inside of my neck all the way out and down the top of my arm. I swayed slightly because his touch was so incredible.

"Your skin is cold," he murmured, his lips brushing against my flesh when he spoke.

I didn't feel cold. I felt the farthest thing from it. Not being able to take another second of not touching him, I wrapped my hand around his bicep and marveled at the hardness of his body compared to mine. It was like he was carved out of stone and I was filled up inside with cotton.

I let my fingers trace over some of the designs displayed on his arm and then traveled down until the tips of my fingers brushed over the inside of his palm. Brody's hand spasmed and closed around mine, and he adjusted his hold so our fingers were linked together.

"Come on," he murmured, towing me along behind him.

Inside the bathroom, he bent down and closed the drain to the large garden tub and then turned on the faucets.

"What are you doing?" I asked.

"You said you wanted to clean up."

"What about you?" I asked, thinking he meant to leave me in here alone while he went to change.

"Oh, I'm very dirty too."

A little thrill shot through me and ended right in my core. Moisture began to pool between my thighs as my body started to ache for him.

"What about this?" I asked, skimming fingers along the edge of the bandage at his side.

"We'll just have to keep the water level low," he murmured, stepping close and wrapping his arm around my bare waist. "But don't worry. I'll make sure you get good and wet."

My insides trembled because I knew he wasn't talking about the water, and I liked it. As warm water filled the bottom of the tub, Brody's fingers found the hooks at the back of my bra and deftly undid the clasp. Because the fabric was still wet, it stuck to my skin instead of instantly falling away.

The tips of his fingers started at the center of my back and dragged around, over my ribcage, and delved under the edges of the material. I shuddered when he brushed against the underside of my breast and worked his way up to peel away the damp fabric and bare my chest completely.

The sound of a breath expelling from deep within him excited me, making me feel like what he saw pleased him, and yes, I definitely wanted to please him.

Using both his hands, he cupped my naked breasts, weighing them in his palms and tweaking the rock-hard nipples that puckered in the center.

I bit my lip to keep from crying out. He had yet to really touch me, and already I was so worked up I could barely stand still.

"I love your shape," he murmured, letting his hands float down the sides of my waist and then hook into the waistband of my leggings.

"You're the perfect mix of curves and flesh. This part, right here," he whispered, grabbing the area just above my hips, "is a perfect fit for my hands. It's exactly where I plan to hold you when you sink your heat down over my cock and ride me 'til you scream."

The picture that painted caused the inner muscles deep in my vagina to spasm with desperation. Just the thought of him filling me up inside and allowing me to have the control of moving over him was enough to get me to orgasm right here in front of him.

I shivered when he peeled away my leggings and panties, and I swooned when he bent down at my feet to work the damp clothes over my ankles, then tossed them aside. Instead of standing up immediately, Brody wrapped his hands around my ankles and slid upward, touching every last inch of my legs, pausing at the sensitive flesh behind my knees, giving it an extra stroke. I couldn't stop my legs from trembling. I was like a newborn calf, standing there naked before him, wobbly and unsteady.

Brody kept sliding upward around to the front of my thighs, traveling to the sensitive, secret area where my body met my legs.

"A natural redhead," he murmured, tangling his fingers in the sort, groomed curls at the apex of my hips. He dipped his thumb, sliding into the slit of my body and making brief contact with the swollen, throbbing knob buried beneath the folds.

I reached out and grabbed the wall, no longer able to stand fully upright.

I heard his pleased chuckle, and he abandoned my body to stand up and draw me into the circle of his arms. "I'll support you," he murmured, lowering his head and taking my lips.

He coaxed my mouth open with deep, even kisses and then swept that devilish tongue right inside my mouth, twisting around my tongue and making me melt against his bare chest.

We were skin to skin, body to body. The cold button at the waistband of his jeans dug into my lower abdomen, and I pushed against it, my body desperate for some kind of pressure.

In that moment I wished I was taller because the hard length of him straining against his jeans was exactly what I wanted to feel at my core, but it was too high for me to rub against. I made a frustrated sound into his mouth and the kiss broke with his wide smile.

He pulled away and placed his hands beneath my arms, lifting me as if I weighed no more than a feather, and set me down into the tub, which was filling with deliciously warm water. I sank down into the silky heat and sighed.

Brody turned off the faucet before the water level could get too high and then he popped the button on his jeans. I watched with heavy limbs as he pulled off the pants and boxer briefs he wore.

His penis was thick and jutted out from beneath a neat nest of short, dark curls, pointing at me like it knew exactly who it belonged to.

I had the perfect view of his entire package as he stood beside the tub, staring down at me as warm water lapped at my skin. His balls were full and heavy, the skin much more delicate looking than the taut casing covering his unbending length.

Without hesitation, I reached up and cupped them in my palm, rolling them around in my fingers and caressing the underside with delicate, light strokes. Brody shuddered and his body jerked. I smiled and dragged my nails down the inside of his thigh.

A low growl filled the air, and I scooted back so there was plenty of room for him to join me.

The water level rose considerably when he lowered his bulky, cut, tattooed form down beside me. Water splashed up his sides and teased the bottom edges of the bandage covering his wound.

"There's too much water." I worried, reaching behind me for the stopper, to drain out some of the water.

"Leave it," he commanded, grabbing my hand and bringing it back around.

"But—"

He shook his head, cutting off my words, and pulled me closer. My bare bottom slid over the smooth floor of the tub and my body came right up against him. His legs were spread so I fit between them, and when I was close enough, he wrapped his calves around my back, caging me in so I was totally surrounded by him.

Brody slid the bands out of the ends of my completely ruined braids and tossed them over the edge. Slowly, he worked his fingers through the tangles in my hair until the length of it trailed down my back and the ends fell into the water.

"Lean back," he instructed, and it took a moment for me to maneuver because he didn't move his legs. So I draped my body over him, thrusting my chest up into the sky as my head and shoulders fell back and my hair soaked up the warm water.

I felt him reach forward, bending over me as he worked the water into the entire length of my hair. My eyes slid closed because his touch felt so wonderful.

His mouth closed over one of my bared breasts, and his chest came into contact with my core. My body jerked because my legs were spread around him, and the most sensitive spot on my entire body rubbed against him, making me moan.

Brody drew my nipple into his mouth, sucking firmly, while holding the mound of flesh securely in place. I couldn't stop myself from rubbing against his chest. The friction between my body and his was absolutely luscious.

Before I could get too out of control with my movements, he sat back and lifted me up with him. I watched with heavy eyes as he moved the thick, wet mass over one side of my shoulder and away from the bandage I somehow managed to keep dry. He dumped some shampoo in his palm and then worked it into my hair, massaging my scalp and making me purr.

The suds dripped down over my shoulder and ran down my body. Just the very light sensation of the bubbles made my body tighten with even more need.

When he was done washing, he tilted me back once more so he could rinse out all the soap. He watched as I wrung out the moisture, letting it fall into the water, and then twisted it into a topknot and tucked the ends under to keep the heavy weight of it from dripping on my bandage.

Nearby was a bar of soap and I picked it up, dipping it into the water and lathering up my hands. Still sitting between his spread thighs, I smoothed the soap over his chest and shoulders. I washed him carefully, trying to avoid his bandage but realizing it was already wet. I couldn't bring myself to worry because there was no room in my body for those kinds of thoughts right now. I was so stuffed with desire and yearning that I could barely breathe, let alone think.

My hand slid lower, over the cut ridges of his abdominals and across the narrow side of his waist.

When my hand met the top of his manhood, I raised my eyes, almost as if asking for permission to go farther.

In response, his eyes slid shut and his hips tilted upward. I took my slick hand and ran down to the base of his penis. I squeezed gently around the base, marveling at the thickness and strength of his erection. I shivered lightly when I imagined what it would feel like to have something so stiff in the center of my body.

Using one hand, I began to stroke him with slow up and down movements as my other hand found the underside of his sack, which was now tight and closer to his body.

I worked them simultaneously, trying to give him as much pleasure as I knew how.

God, he was so beautiful. His body was wide and smooth, his waist tapered into slim hips, and that V between his hips and scrotum was pretty much the sexiest indent I had ever seen. The tattoos that covered his body were mostly black and abstract designs, and they stretched over the firmness of his muscles, making his entire body look like the perfect canvas for such art.

Even though he wasn't touching me, even though his fingers didn't tease my core, I felt my body urging higher and higher, like an orgasm was near. Just looking at him, just letting my hands roam over him, was enough to bring me to the peak of pleasure.

His hand came down to still mine, and he lifted his head and stared at me with a drunk look across his features. "My turn," he murmured, his voice sounding like he ate a bucket of gravel.

The next thing I knew, he was sliding his soapy hands over every single inch of my body. He paid more attention to some areas than others, but I wasn't about to complain.

The desire and need he withdrew from me was so thick that it coated the insides of my thighs so fully that not even the water in the bath could wash it away.

When he was satisfied I was clean, he drew me close, spinning me in the circle of his body and draping my back against his chest. With the back of my head pillowed on his shoulder, both his arms snaked around to my front and delved down below the water and into my folds.

Unabashedly, I spread my legs, propping my feet up on either side of the tub. I was too far gone for modesty. I was too far gone to act like this wasn't practically heaven on Earth.

Every time he touched the ultra-sensitive, ultra-swollen and wet clit, my body jerked. I couldn't control it. It was like he found a secret button that caused my body to act involuntarily to his will.

"You want to come, don't you?" he whispered in my ear.

God, yes, I did.

But I also liked the sweet torture of that bliss being just out of reach.

"You can come now, Taylor," he murmured. "Because when you're done, I will just make you come again."

I moaned as two of his fingers slid deep inside me and his thumb started rubbing against my clit.

My body arched up and away from his as I momentarily went deaf and blind. I felt myself moaning and calling out his name, but I didn't hear. I didn't see the light-colored walls or any of my surroundings.

All I could do was ride the wave of pleasure that completely took over my body.

It went on and on and on. Just when I thought I was going to stop falling, he would move his fingers again and a renewed wave of bliss would shake my body.

Finally, my body seemed to come back to life and I collapsed against him in a trembling heap. Brody tried to withdrawal his fingers, but I squeezed my thighs closed. I wasn't ready for him to leave me yet. I wasn't ready for my insides to be empty.

I lay there trying to catch my breath as he chuckled and pressed a soft kiss against the side of my temple.

The stiff, unyielding flesh at my back poked into me, demanding equal treatment. I wanted to give him the same kind of ethereal pleasure he gave to me so I let him pull away and I sat up, swaying a little as I tried to support my own weight.

I reached for him, but he stood abruptly, pulling a white towel off the nearby rack and crudely drying off before wrapping it around his waist. I gave him a hard, unhappy glare, and he smiled a slow, wolfishly charming smile.

"Oh, I'm not done with you yet," he said. "But I want you beneath me."

I climbed out of the tub with wobbly knees as he wrapped a towel around me. He pulled me close and kissed me, wrapping himself around me and walking until we were in the bedroom and the backs of my legs came up against the mattress.

With quick movements, he flung the blankets on the bed back and tossed both our towels on the floor, pushing me down on the bed.

I draped my naked body across the width of the bed, spreading my legs and inviting him in. I'd never in my entire life wanted someone so badly as I did right then.

He prowled onto the mattress, climbing over me and staring down with eyes so dark they looked like the midnight sky. I felt the tip of him push against my entrance and I sighed with anticipation. I bent my knees and tilted my pelvis up to meet him as he surged into me with one long, hard stroke.

I gasped and grabbed fistfuls of the sheets on either side of my hips. Holy crap, he was large. He filled me to capacity and I felt my body stretch out and mold around him, my slick heat coating his bare cock so he could move with ease.

I heard him swallow. His desire was so thick I heard it scrape down his throat. I lifted my eyes so I could look at him, and he stilled. He didn't start to pump into me. He didn't spear me over and over again with his unyielding thickness.

He gazed down at me tenderly, like he could care less about achieving an orgasm. His eyes swept over my features with a small amount of wonderment. His hand came up to brush away a few stray strand of hair from my face, and he smiled. My heart literally did a somersault right beneath my ribs.

His lips brushed mine, once, twice, and then a third time. His tender kisses were the complete opposite of his throbbing cock trying to remain still deep within my body.

Brody trailed light kisses across my cheek, to the corner of my eye, and then to the tip of my nose. I sighed as he levered himself above me, balancing his weight on his arms, and then he started to move.

He wasn't gentle, but it didn't hurt. Over and over again he speared me with what could only be described as an unyielding sword. Every single plunge he made had me crying out and begging for more.

I couldn't think of anything other than the way it felt as he drove inside me.

Just when I thought I couldn't take any more, he pushed so deep our pelvis bones ground together. My insides quivered as he began to grind against me, keeping himself buried to the hilt.

My breath came in short gasps until I was literally panting with need.

Brody's body went rigid and a cry ripped from his throat. He pushed up inside me even farther, and I was sure I felt the tip of his length brush against the bottom of my belly. With one final swivel of his hips, an orgasm burst through me and I cried out, unable to form a single word, not even his name.

I don't know how long I floated between bliss and reality, but I didn't care. I didn't even realize my body was capable of those kinds of feelings, that pleasure like this even existed.

Eventually, he collapsed onto the mattress beside me but rolled and pulled me into his body. The sticky warmth he left between my legs coated my thighs, but I was in no hurry to get up and wipe it away. If anything, I liked the way it felt.

In fact, there wasn't one thing about Brody West that I didn't like.

19

Brody

Holy. Freaking. Hell.

This one time, I went to a club and was dragged by triplets (okay, I went willingly) into the private owner's section in the back.

Three smoking-hot, identical, dark-haired sexual wizards.

They did things to my body that I still dreamed about today. I mean, think about it: three mouths, three sets of hands, and three overeager ladies willing and ready to do anything to please me.

It was the best sexual experience of my entire life.

Until now.

How this single girl could outdo three women (at once!) was not something to be taken lightly. She was a siren. She was a witch... Just how much experience did this little vixen have?

The thought made my blood run cold. It actually made me angry, turned my insides rigid. The thought of her doing any of this to anyone else made me see red. I would murder him.

I moved quickly, the thought literally taking over my brain and fueling me on. I rolled, pinning her to the mattress and giving her a solid stare. "I need to know something."

Her eyes widened and she nodded.

"How many have there been before me?"

Her perfect little mouth opened in an O. Wariness seeped into her eyes, and I fought the urge to scowl.

Forget every respectful thought I previously had about her father.

He should have kept a better eye on her. Someone like her practically needed constant supervision.

"Why would you ask me that?" she said, a little wrinkle appearing between her brows.

"I need to know," I ground out. Just lying on her like this was making my cock stir with renewed desire. Even anger at someone else's hands on her wasn't enough to keep my manhood from swelling from her closeness.

Her eyes turned shiny and she looked away. "Was it that bad for you?"

She sucked in a breath as the hurt in her voice socked me in the gut. "What?" I asked incredulously. She couldn't possibly think I hadn't enjoyed that.

"I'm not very experienced. I—" she began, her voice tearful, her eyes still turned away.

Relief like no other poured through me. But so did regret. I hadn't meant to hurt her with my question. I caught her chin and turned her face so I could look into her eyes. "Stop right there," I said gently. "This was by far the best I've ever had. *You* are the best I've ever had."

"Really?" she whispered.

God, her vulnerability was going to be my undoing. I'd never in all my years ever met a woman so capable of tying me up in the most impossible knots. She was a tomboy yet girly. She was rich, but not spoiled. She was inexperienced but made me insane with need.

"I didn't mean to make you think I wasn't satisfied, sweetheart," I murmured, stroking the hair away from her face. "I've never been so satisfied, and it's made me crazy."

The emerald of her eyes shone a little as I spoke.

"The thought of you doing that with anyone else… Well, I won't lie. It's got me thinking about murder."

She giggled like my confession of wanting to kill was something she was charmed by.

"How many, Tay?" I asked again. I had to know.

"A few." She hedged. "But it's never been like this."

"Never?"

She shook her head. "The first was in high school. We had no idea what we were doing and it really wasn't that great." She made a face like she was grossed out, and it pleased me to no end. "The second was in college, but the only time he ever wanted to do it was when he was drunk… It sort of made me feel like I wasn't that attractive when he was sober."

"Douche," I muttered. "He was probably gay."

She laughed and her belly vibrated against my chest. It made me smile.

"And then there was someone a couple years ago… We might have been more serious, but when my mother died, I pulled away. I just didn't have it in me to be in a relationship at that time in my life."

"Makes sense," I whispered, rubbing my thumb across her lower lip.

"And now there's you."

"I'm the best," I said, cocky. Now that I knew there was no one I needed to kill, I felt a lot better.

"You definitely are." She agreed.

I kissed her deeply and lay back down, taking her with me.

I felt her stiffen a little and I realized I likely tugged her arm. I sat up and stared down, lifting the bandaged area and checking it to make sure nothing was wet, bleeding, or coming loose.

"It stayed almost completely dry," she said.

"How long's it been since you've had your pain meds?"

"Since this morning."

I frowned. After all the movement and activity at the lake and then here in bed, she needed to rest it. She needed her meds and that sling back in place. If she kept moving around this much, it was going to get even sorer and take longer to heal. I pulled away. "Come on. We need to get you taken care of."

She made a sound of protest. "I don't wanna get up."

I grinned lazily. "There's more where that came from." I leaned down and kissed her. "But what the hell kind of man would I be if I neglected my girl's wounds?"

"Your girl?" she said, looking up at me from amongst the twisted blankets and sheets.

I'd never claimed anyone as solely mine before. I never really cared. But claiming her was as natural as breathing. I didn't even have to think about it.

She was like finally finding home.

I hooked my hand around her ankle and slowly towed her across the bed toward me. "Yeah, mine."

"Does that mean you're mine?"

"Do you want me?" The question kind of ripped from my throat, like it was sticky. It was hard to put myself out there like that, to practically lay out my vulnerabilities at her feet.

"I want you very much," she whispered, reaching out her hand.

I took it and towed her up onto her feet, bringing her naked, luscious body against mine. I flattened my palm against the back of her head and hugged her against me. I wasn't sure how this happened. How I went from a solitary man to a guy who needed someone else.

And I did need her.

In the beginning, I might have felt the weight of responsibility by having her around, but nothing about her now seemed heavy. If anything, she made me feel lighter.

It was a little unsettling for this to happen so fast.

She laughed and pulled back. "Your stomach is growling like an angry bear."

I grabbed her ass. "I worked up an appetite."

Taylor rolled her eyes and pulled away. "Let's get dressed and go down to the kitchen."

My chest swelled with some sort of strong emotion as I watched her hips sway into the bathroom. Yes, things between Taylor and me definitely moved fast.

I thought about applying the brakes, about slowing things down.

From inside the bathroom, she dropped something and called herself an idiot. I smiled.

To hell with brakes.

The blow-dryer kicked on, and I unzipped my duffle to find some clothes. On top of the pile was my cell phone. I forgot to turn up the volume when we came inside. I picked it up and lit up the screen. A missed call flashed in front of me so I pulled up the info and hit redial.

"Newman," the man answered after only one ring.

"It's West. Sorry I missed your call before."

"Not a problem. I just wanted to let you know that we brought in Snake about an hour ago."

"Fucking right," I said happily. "He being booked now?"

"Yeah, then we'll put him in lockup."

"Hey, man, I appreciate the call. Thanks for bringing him in. Good work."

After we disconnected the call, I tossed the phone and reached for a pair of clean boxer briefs. I thought about the fact I should be on Emerald Isle right now, fishing. I should be sitting in the sand with nothing to think about other than what to eat for dinner.

How quickly things could change.

After the bust at the gas station went down, I still planned to get the hell out of town for my two-week vacation. I didn't plan on thinking about the job or where I was going to live. But all that changed when I stepped into Taylor's hospital room and realized I couldn't just walk away from her.

And now here I was, thinking about getting a place of my own, about sticking around and figuring out what my life looked like without a second identity.

That is if I lived long enough for any of that.

Now that word was out about my undercover identity, members of the crew, people from my past, were going to come looking for me, and they weren't gonna want to have dinner and a movie. They would come with the hopes of putting me in a grave.

The blow-dryer in the bathroom clicked off and Taylor's soft humming drifted out into the bedroom.

Her father asked me to be here to protect her. It's why I came.

But now my presence could be nothing but dangerous.

I thought about that as I yanked on a pair of jeans and a navy-blue T-shirt from Old Navy. The wound in my side was sore and I glanced down, remembering that the bandage covering the stitches hadn't stayed dry in the tub. I grabbed one corner of the bandage and ripped it off in one sweeping motion. The skin burned, but I ignored it.

After I made sure the stitches themselves looked okay, I discarded the bandage and let my shirt fall over it. Band-Aids were a pain in the ass and I was tired of wearing one.

Taylor stepped into the room and lightly padded over toward the bed. She was dressed in a pair of darkly colored jeans that molded to her every curve. Her T-shirt was dark purple, loose, and had a large teal-colored peace sign on the front. Her long, red locks were dry and tangle free. The straight strands hung way down to the middle of her back and seemed to capture and reflect light with every move she made. It was tucked casually behind her ears, almost like the way she looked was an afterthought.

As I stared, she lifted up the scattered blankets near the end of the bed and reached for her sling.

"Here," I said, taking it from her hands and fastening it around her. Very gently, I helped her guide her arm into the contraption and then made sure it was adjusted to fit her body.

When I was done, she looked up and smiled.

My fingers found hers, intertwining and leading her from the room.

Yeah, my presence was dangerous to her. But I spent the last several years of my professional life walking away from people who would be better off without me. It was isolating and in some ways made me feel like the person I had been was slowly evaporating until there would be nothing left. Then one day I would look in a mirror and see nothing but a stranger.

I was tired of doing that. I didn't want to be a threat to Taylor's safety, but I didn't want to give her up either.

I needed to do some damage control.

20

Taylor

I couldn't stop watching him. Everything about the way he moved enticed me. The way his fingers wrapped around the end of the fork reminded me what they felt like on my skin. The way his lips closed over the food and the little moan of appreciation from his throat made me think about what it had been like to lie beneath his naked body.

"Am I gonna need to feed you again?" he said, not looking away from his heaping plate of French toast bake. The affection in his voice warmed me better than any cup of coffee ever could.

"I'm not really that hungry," I said, watching the way his Adam's apple bobbed in his throat. I hadn't eaten in hours, but I was thoroughly satisfied.

After shoving another humungous bite of food into his mouth, he dropped the fork, allowing it to clatter against the plate. Then he spun on the stool he was sitting on to face me. Gently, he pulled the coffee mug out of my hands and set it aside. His arm brushed the inside of my leg when he grasped the edge of the

[200]

stool and dragged it across the floor, bringing my chair right up against his.

Keeping his eyes on me, he lifted my legs so they were spread and rested on either side of his hips and he was right between my thighs. "How's a man supposed to get anything done when his woman stares at him with desire written all over her face?" he asked softly, delving his fingers into my hair and pulling me in for a kiss.

He tasted like syrup, sweet and sinful. I licked into his mouth and the flavor of cinnamon burst over my tongue. His mouth was warm and giving, making me feel wanted and welcome.

As we kissed, he pulled his fingers through my hair, winding a few strands around his hand and rubbing a thumb along my collarbone. I'd never felt so connected to anyone in my entire life. It didn't feel as if we'd just met, but that I'd known him for years. He wasn't the kind of guy I ever thought I would get involved with, but the more time I spent with him, I realized he was exactly the kind of guy I needed.

Brody was the kind of guy who would challenge me. He wasn't predictable like the numbers I worked with on a daily basis. He was a math equation without a definitive answer. He was a dash of salt in my otherwise bland day.

I didn't know everything about him, I didn't know what the future held for us, but I was looking forward to finding out.

He pulled back and studied me with chocolate eyes. "I probably shouldn't be here right now," he said, brushing my hair behind my shoulder. "This is the most selfish thing I've ever done."

"Why?" I curled my fingers into the hem of his T-shirt.

"I'm putting you in danger, Tay. Snake's been running his mouth, probably telling everyone who would listen that I'm not who they thought I was. I'm going to have a target on my back. They're going to come after me. The only thing worse than a cop is a cop who pretends to be one of their own."

Concern squeezed my chest, but it wasn't concern for myself. It was for him. I realized then that dating a cop, being with someone who was constantly in harm's way, wasn't going to be easy. I would wonder about him every day, if he was safe, if he would come home to me.

He placed a finger beneath my chin and forced my gaze up. "Hey," he said quietly. "I'll leave. I'll walk out of here right now if that's what you want."

"Would it really be so easy for you?" I whispered, an ache in my chest. Yes, it had only been days since he pretty much crashed into my life, but even so, if he walked away, I would feel his absence profoundly.

"No," he answered. "But staying here and hurting you would be worse."

This is how I knew he was the kind of man I needed. He was giving me a choice. He wasn't making a decision about us without me. And if I asked him to leave, he would because he would respect what I wanted. My fingers tightened in his shirt, tugging the fabric across his back and pulling him closer. "I don't want you to leave."

Brody untangled my hand from his shirt and lifted it to press a kiss to the palm of my hand before wrapping it up in his own.

Was it possible to want someone just minutes after you had them? Was it possible that the warmth sliding through my abdomen was renewed desire? Lust was a powerful emotion, and it was obvious I lusted after Brody.

Outside of the kitchen, I heard a key in the door, the lock slide free, and it push open. Brody stiffened, all his attention going to the doorway between the room we were sitting in and the small entryway off the garage.

Seconds later, my father walked in, his tie slightly askew and a briefcase in his hand.

"Hi, Dad," I said, and he looked up, surprise written on his face. He gave me a warm smile that quickly faded as he took in the close proximity of Brody and me.

"How are you feeling?" he asked, giving Brody a pointed look.

Brody pretended he didn't see it and kept himself exactly where he was. It pleased me. Not because I wanted to disrespect my father in his own house, but because I liked that Brody wasn't intimidated by him. Too many guys were scared away by the prospect of dealing with an overprotective, resource-rich father.

"I'm feeling good," I said, getting down from the stool to go around the island. "Can I make you a sandwich?"

"That would be great," he said, finally looking away from Brody and setting his briefcase on the counter. "I didn't have time to eat today."

I busied myself getting out everything I needed to make ham and turkey sandwiches, and my father busied himself questioning Brody.

"I see you've been watching over my daughter."

"I told you I would."

[203]

"Dad." I butted in. "You seriously offered to pay Brody to be my bodyguard?"

"He's qualified for the position."

I sighed. "You know how I feel about you trying to manage my life."

"I will not lose you," he replied. "You're all I have left."

Pain pierced my heart and I gave up the argument. My mother's death had been very difficult for my father. She was the love of his life, and when she finally succumbed to the cancer, a part of him died with her. It was maddening as hell the way he tried to protect me, but I couldn't bring myself to be angry at him.

"I told you I didn't want your money," Brody said, looking at my father. "This isn't about money for me."

"What's it about, then?" Dad challenged.

"Her," he said simply.

Dad looked like he swallowed something sour, and I knew he would likely say something next about how Brody wasn't good enough for his daughter. *That* would make me mad.

"Snake was brought into custody a little while ago," I said quickly, before the conversation could turn unpleasant.

Dad glanced at me. "Well, that's good news." He looked over at Brody. "I guess your services aren't needed anymore."

I sighed.

Brody didn't seem the least bit offended. "Well, since I wasn't really working for you, you can't fire me."

The sour look appeared again, and I hurried to slide a sandwich in front of him.

The sound of a ringing cell phone cut into the conversation. *Thank God.* Brody stood up and dug his cell out of his pocket.

"West," he answered briskly.

I gave my father a pointed look, hoping he would hear my silent plea to behave when Brody finished his call.

"Got it. I'll be there," he said and then disconnected the call and deposited the phone back into his pants. After he slid the stool back under the counter and forked the last heaping bite of French toast on his plate into his mouth, he looked up. "I have some paperwork at the station."

Disappointment was a sharp taste in my mouth. I didn't want him to go.

Brody helped himself to a gulp of my coffee and then came around the side of the counter and kissed the side of my head. "I'll check on you later."

"'Kay."

"You have my number, right?"

I nodded.

"Get some rest, Tay."

I liked when he called me that.

"Edward," he said by way of good-bye to my father, who only nodded.

When he was gone, Dad gave me a knowing look.

"At least you know he's above bribery," I said.

"I still don't like him," he replied and took a bite of his sandwich.

I smiled. He liked him. He just didn't want to admit it.

21

Brody

I lied.

It wasn't hard.

I didn't even feel guilty for it.

I'd do it again. Yeah, I told Taylor the risks of spending time with me. I gave her a choice. I wanted her to know what she was walking into if she accepted any kind of relationship with me.

It was probably wrong.

I probably shouldn't have given her a choice at all. But I wasn't going to be that guy. I wasn't going to think I knew what was best for her. And, like I told her, I was selfish.

I knew she wouldn't walk away from me. The chemistry between us was too good. For the first time ever in my life, I was taking something I really wanted and I planned to keep it.

And so I lied.

I wasn't about to put Taylor at any more risk than absolutely necessary. I did have paperwork to do at the station. But that wasn't why I was going there.

Newman called. The perp was asking for me. He wouldn't talk to anyone else. And I wanted to talk to him.

Talking to him = plowing my fist in his face.

Would it get me in trouble?

Yep.

Did I give a rat's ass?

Nope.

Snake deserved way worse than I was going to be able to deliver in a ten-by-ten interrogation room. Besides, I wanted answers. I intended to get them. I needed to know how far and how wide he blasted my identity. I needed to know what kind of cleanup I was facing.

I wasn't going to live with a cloud of retaliation over my head. I wasn't going to look over my shoulder and wonder if Taylor was going to get caught in the crossfire.

The only way to do that was to make sure all the roads that led to me were dead.

The inside of the police station was fairly quiet, but given that it was almost dark out, I wasn't really surprised. There were still many uniformed men behind their desks and a receptionist answering the phone. On my way in, I winked at her and she blushed.

Some of the officers looked at me curiously as I made my way past, but no one bothered to stop me from going straight to Mac's office.

I didn't know all the guys that worked here. I'd been undercover too long to really form relationships with a lot of them. The ones I did know all had their own partners and routines that I didn't fit in with. I didn't mind not fitting in. In fact, it was that quality that made me good at being undercover.

It was always the misfits who seemed to turn to a life in the organization.

After a swift courtesy knock on his door, I opened it and walked in. He was sitting behind his desk, frowning at the computer screen. He grunted when he looked up. "'Bout damn time you got here. You sure took your sweet-ass time coming in to give your statement and fill out paperwork on today's latest shootout."

"I thought I was still on vacation."

"Christ," Mac swore. "Everywhere you go, West, there seems to be a shootout."

"What can I say?" I shrugged. "I'm charming."

He made a rude sound that I filed away for later (I was going to use that one), and he scowled at the computer. "What ever happened to just doing shit by hand?" he muttered.

I grinned.

"The perp's asking for me?"

"Yep. I told him he could talk with whoever I sent in the room." He shook his head. "Damn criminals these days think they can come in here and call the shots."

"I need five minutes with him."

Mac gave me a level stare. "It's not a good idea."

"Probably not." I agreed.

"No."

"I need to know how many people he told about my identity."

Mac swore. "You know as well as I do he ain't gonna tell you the truth."

Most likely, no. But that didn't mean I wasn't going to beat the truth out of him. I kept that little tidbit of information to myself.

"Maybe since he's been lying low, he hasn't had time to tell that many people. We already got the guys who tried to kill me today so we know they aren't talking. We might be able to keep a lid on this."

"You know your undercover career is over, don't you?" he said quietly.

"Yes. Which is exactly why I want to see him. I have to make sure I can have a real life where I don't have to look over my shoulder."

"We could transfer you," he suggested. "Get you out of here."

Any other time I would have taken the transfer and moved on. Yeah, I had family not too far away, but my relationship with them had faded away a long time ago. There wasn't really anything to keep me here.

Until Taylor.

"I'm not running," I growled.

"It's the girl, isn't it?"

I stared at him in stony silence.

"Taylor Shaw," he said.

I crossed my arms over my chest.

He whistled between his teeth. "You got it bad, don't ya? You know her daddy is a powerful, rich man in this town."

"Edward Shaw does not intimidate me."

Mac grinned because I pretty much just confirmed what he was implying. When I offered no more information on my personal life, he wiped a hand down his face.

"Five minutes."

I smiled and turned to leave.

"West."

I stopped but didn't turn back.

"Keep your hands to yourself. Don't force me to suspend you. You're one of the best on the PD."

I left the room without response. I wasn't going to make a promise I couldn't keep. Out in the hall, Newman was passing by with a folder full of papers. "He's down the hall."

"What's he been saying?"

"He won't say shit. Says he'll only talk to you," Newman spat. "He keeps grinning like he has some big secret. We've sent three guys in there already and all of them have come out wanting to punch out someone's lights."

Weariness smacked me in the gut. Shit, I was tired. All the games that went into this kind of life were starting to wear on me. The damn media actually did me a favor when they outed me. I was tired of being undercover. I was glad this was the end of that chapter in my life. Moving on sounded like a pretty good idea.

I paused outside the interrogation room and took a breath, reminding myself to keep my cool. The reminder was likely useless. If he pushed me too far, I wouldn't be keeping my hands to myself.

The door flung wide when I walked in, smacking against the wall with a loud crack, and then swung shut. Snake was sitting at the table with his back turned to me and he jumped from the sudden burst of sound and movement.

"I heard you've been asking for me," I said, stepping farther into the room to walk around the table.

Snake didn't say anything. His dark head just lounged lazily in the chair like being under arrest was nothing to worry about. He was still dressed in the same T-shirt and jeans from the day I met him at the bank.

"Let me tell you how this is going to work," I said, slapping my hand down on the table and looking ahead at the dirty wall. "I'm going to ask you some questions and you're going to answer. If you don't, I'll make your life a living hell in this place. If you do, maybe I'll see about sending you to the cushy prison upstate."

That was a lie. I was going to make sure he went to a hellhole and had a roommate named Tiny.

"How about you do the listening?" he replied.

There was something about his voice… something that wasn't quite right.

I whipped around, focusing on his face.

He started to laugh.

My blood ran cold and a strange buzzing sound filled my head. I stood there staring at him, suddenly understanding exactly why he seemed so unworried about being arrested.

This was not Snake.

He was the same height and build. He had the same coloring and he was wearing Snake's clothes. But this wasn't the guy who masterminded the robbery on Shaw's Trust. This wasn't the guy who tried to kill me. Who tried to kill Taylor.

Rage lit within me like a candle to a flame. I burst forward and grabbed up the decoy by the collar of his shirt, yanking him out of the chair and lifting him off the ground.

"What the hell is this?" I growled.

He grinned, his breathing coming in uneven bursts. "Payback."

I slammed him down on the table, making it rattle under his weight. I enjoyed the way his head bounced off the tabletop and his eyes registered surprise.

"You can't touch me," he said, his smile slipping just a little bit.

I smiled. "That's where you're wrong." Holding him down, I plowed my fist into the side of his jaw. The force of the hit sent him sliding off the table and onto the floor.

He scrambled up, blood spilling down his chin. "He said you had to play by the rules, that as a cop you couldn't do shit but release me," the kid said, fear coming into his eyes as he backed away from me.

"He lied."

Decoy Snake's eyes grew wide and his back hit the wall. He was a lot younger looking than the actual Snake, and he was too green to know to hide his anxiety. I slapped my hands against the wall on either side of his head.

"Lying to a police officer, giving false information, conspiring with a known criminal," I listed. "All legit offenses. You could do some jail time for this."

His eyes bulged.

"Don't worry. You're young and you got that innocent look going on. I'm sure the Tinys and the Butches of the prison will take a liking to you and protect you." I leaned a little bit closer to whisper, "In exchange for favors, of course."

"I didn't do nothing!" he burst out, trying to push me away.

I stepped back and he tried to rush past me toward the door. I grabbed him by the sleeve of his shirt and hauled him back, slamming him against the wall. My hand closed over his throat, applying just enough pressure so he knew I wasn't fucking around.

"How many people did Snake tell my real identity?"

"I don't know," he said, his voice strained.

I squeezed harder. "How. Many?"

He gagged and clawed at my hand. I didn't release him and I didn't loosen my grip. I just stared at him, waiting.

"Not many!" he wheezed.

I lightened my grip and he gulped in great heaves of oxygen. "How many is not many?"

"I don't know, man," he said, leaning against the wall. Sweat had broken out across his forehead. "There weren't many of us in the room. Just me and four other guys."

There were three guys at the lake today. "He put out a hit on me?"

He nodded. "Three guys never came back."

"That's because I killed one and threw the other two in jail," I growled.

"He said you were a spineless cop!" he burst out. "He said once we got rid of you, he'd make me second-in-command for doing this!"

Now we were getting somewhere. So it seemed Snake only had a small crew on his payroll. Most of which were now in jail. The rest of his would-be crewmembers were likely still scrambling from all the previous busts. Maybe word hadn't gotten out as much as I thought. Maybe there was a chance to keep my identity mostly contained.

I tossed the kid on the floor and he lay there gasping for air, his cheeks bright red. "Where is he?" I asked.

"I can't tell you," he cried. "Please. If I tell you, he'll kill me."

"If you don't tell me, *I'll* kill you."

He seemed to recover some of his earlier bravado. "You won't. You wouldn't dare kill me in the middle of a police station."

I pulled the gun I was carrying out of the waistband of my jeans. It wasn't my waterlogged .45, but a pistol.

I pressed the barrel up against his forehead, hard enough to leave a mark. "Are you sure about that?"

He whimpered. "It doesn't matter where he's staying because he's not there."

Warning skittered across the back of my neck. I wasn't asking the right questions right now. I should be asking why he sent a lookalike to be arrested in his place. A lookalike who was instructed to ask for me and only me.

What exactly would he gain from that?

"What is he planning?" I yelled, lifting him off the ground while still pressing the gun to his head.

"I don't know!"

I threw him up against the wall. I heard something inside him crack and he slid to the floor, calling out in pain. I pounced on him.

"Tell me!" I roared, cocking the gun.

The door to the room banged open and three officers rushed in.

"I told you to keep your hands off him!" Mac yelled from the doorway.

I was beyond listening. My finger was getting twitchy on the trigger. The kid must have seen the look in my eyes because he said, "He's going after your weakness. He's going after her."

Taylor.

I jumped to my feet, my insides wild with adrenaline.

"That's not Snake," I spat, pushing my way toward the door. "It's a decoy."

I shoved my way out into the hall and took off running.

"West!" Mac called from behind.

"He's going after Taylor!" I yelled and kept on running.

I shouldn't have let my guard down so fast. I should have followed up when they first brought Snake in here. I'd been set up.

And now Taylor was going to pay the price.

22

Taylor

Dad was only home about thirty minutes when his phone started ringing with something down at the bank demanding attention immediately.

I heard him on the line, trying to work it out so someone else could take care of the matter, as he didn't want to leave me here alone (like I was ten or something). I'd had about enough of his hovering in the past few days to last me a lifetime, and I promptly walked into the room and glared at him until he lowered the phone.

"Do you need something, Taylor?"

"No, Dad, I'm fine. If you're needed at work, just go."

Doubt crept into his eyes, and I sighed. "Snake is in custody. There's no reason why you can't go into work. I'm going to lie down anyway. I'm tired." It wasn't a lie. The pain meds were making my limbs feel heavy, and after everything that happened this morning and then later on (in bed), I really did just want to rest.

"I'll be there shortly," he said into the phone and then cut the line.

I smiled at him.

"Are you sure about this, honey?" he said. "I don't mind staying home. I've been at work all day."

I felt a little guilty because I didn't want him to think I was trying to get rid of him. "If you want to use me as an excuse to stay in, I'll totally support that," I told him mischievously. "You must be tired."

"Well, this robbery definitely has me putting in a lot of hours lately," he said. "I will be glad when the mess is behind us and I can get back to my regular schedule."

"Maybe I could come in and help?" I offered. It was, after all, the business that I would be running someday.

"Absolutely not," he said, his tone final. "You've been through enough. You need to rest that arm. The bank will be there when you're feeling better."

"How about a coffee to go?" I asked.

He nodded. "That would be great."

I went into the kitchen and pulled down another travel mug, remembering the last time I was doing this. Brody had pressed in so close I could feel the hard contours of his body and his comforting heat. I didn't think he could ever get close enough to me. The way he seemed to always disregard my personal space like there were no boundaries between us made my heart race. I smiled secretly to myself. I loved the way he made me feel, like I was the only woman he wanted in his arms.

"Taylor?" my father asked from behind me. I jumped, startled back into reality.

"Sorry," I said, hurrying to pour the still-hot coffee from before. After securing the lid, I handed over the mug.

"You're thinking about him, aren't you?"

"Yes, Dad." I sighed. "You know, I'm well into my twenties. I'm old enough to have a relationship with someone."

"I know." He sounded sad. "But you'll always be my little girl."

"I will. But maybe you could try to be nice to Brody? Maybe try not to scare him off?"

"Well, at least he would be able to protect you," he muttered.

"Nothing is going to happen to me, Dad." I assured him, feeling guilty for not telling him what happened today at the lake. I hated to make him worry any more than he already did. It seemed that ever since we lost Mom, all he did was worry that something would happen to me and he would be left all alone.

I gave him a one-armed hug and he wrapped his arms around me. "I love you, kid."

"I love you too."

"I'll be home as soon as this latest mess is cleaned up," he said, moving toward the door that led into the garage.

"I'll be here."

Even though Snake was in custody, I would probably stay here a few more days, if only to make my father feel better.

Once I was alone, I went into the kitchen and looked around in the cupboards to see if we had the makings for another pumpkin French toast bake. Brody ate the entire thing, and I thought it would be a good idea to have another one ready to go into the oven for tomorrow.

Holding the end of a long loaf of French bread with the hand in the sling and using the other to tear, I got busy throwing bite-sized pieces of bread into a large glass baking dish. My mind wandered to earlier and the time I spent in his arms. He definitely put every other lover I had to shame.

What happened at the bank was horrible, and being shot and scared I might die had been borderline traumatizing, but something good had come out of it.

Meeting Brody.

If I had to choose between being shot or never meeting him, I would take a bullet any day.

Did that mean I was in love?

I wasn't as naïve as I thought I was, but I was definitely in lust. And I liked him… *a lot*. He made me laugh and he was surprisingly easy to be around. If our relationship progressed the way I thought it might, then love wasn't too far off.

Once the egg and milk mixture was whisked together, I grasped the handle on the mixing bowl to pour it over the bread. When the bowl was in midair, the doorbell rang.

I glanced at the clock. It was after eight. Kind of late for someone to be visiting. It rang again, insistently, and I smiled.

It was probably Brody.

The thought of falling asleep in his arms tonight was so extremely enticing. I set down the bowl and went to the door, smiling.

After I threw the lock and cracked the door, an ominous feeling came over me. I moved to slam the door back in place, to call out before I opened it…

But I was too late.

The door was rammed from the other side so forcefully that I went flying backward and fell onto the floor, sliding across the tile and coming up against the bottom stair. I lay there stunned and reached up to feel the back of my head, which took the impact of the stair. It wasn't bleeding, but it still hurt.

A man charged in the front door after me, leaping on top and grabbing my free arm. "Shouldn't have opened the door, bitch." He snarled.

I'd know his voice and face anywhere. He was supposed to be jail. Brody said Snake was arrested. Fear broke out over my skin like a rash, turning me clammy and shaky.

He laughed. "You underestimated me. I like when people do that."

"I thought you were in jail." I gasped as he yanked me up off the floor.

"I wanted you to *think* I was in jail."

I glanced around, looking for something I could use as a weapon. Unfortunately, since we were standing in a foyer, my options were very limited.

But the front door was open. If I could get away, I could run outside and scream for help. "What do you want?" I asked him, looking away from the door so he wouldn't gauge what I was thinking.

"That pig took away my money, my crew… He made me look like a fool! No one will ever follow me now," he spat, dragging me farther into the house.

I tried to dig my heels into the floor. I needed to stay as close to the door as I could.

"So I decided to take something from him. And you seem to be just the thing to take away." He laughed

[220]

as he dragged me toward the kitchen, and frankly, it pissed me off.

I bent at the waist, leaning down to where he was holding me, and sank my teeth into his arm. I bit down so hard I tasted blood. He howled and pushed me away from him, slamming me face first into the wall.

From inside the kitchen, the landline was ringing. It was like a beacon in the dark. Without thought, I raced toward the sound, desperate to get help. Snake rushed after me as I skidded around the island just as the ringing phone cut off.

He lunged forward and I grabbed the closest thing within reach, the bowl of egg mixture. I threw it, the bowl and all, right at his face. It smacked into his chest, the mixture splattering all over him and then falling to the floor where the glass shattered.

He cursed and I grabbed the phone, skirting around his grabby hands and pressing the number for 9-1-1.

As he slid in the mess I created, I lunged around him, desperate to get to the open front door.

I almost made it.

He caught the hem of my shirt and yanked. My foot caught on some of the spilled eggs on the floor and I went flying, landing hard on my butt.

I gasped, the wind whooshing from my lungs, and my arm groaned from the impact of the fall. The phone flew out of my hand and skidded across the tile just as the operator picked up the line.

"Help!" I screamed. "Help me!"

Snake jumped on me. He looked like some kind of swamp monster with the orange-colored goop all over his face and dripping down the front of his shirt. A gun appeared in his hand, and I struggled anew, slapping at him with my free arm and kicking my legs.

He reached back and slapped me hard across the face. My cheek stung and my eyes watered from the assault. I blinked, desperately willing away the pain when he held the gun down, leveling right at my head.

"Any last words?" he said, giving me a psychotic grin.

Beneath my arm I felt the jagged edge of a piece of the shattered bowl. I wrapped my fingers around it and, with a battle cry, launched myself up and off the floor, swinging my arm around and catching him in the face.

He screamed and dropped the gun, slapping his hand over the cut, which was now oozing blood. I bucked him off and scrambled to get up, slipping a little in the mess but managing to make it to my feet.

At the same time, both of us saw the gun lying there between us. We dove at it, but he was faster, closing his hand around the barrel.

To hell with this.

I slammed the heel of my hand down on his head, knocking his forehead into the floor, and then took off running toward the front of the house.

"Taylor!" Brody bellowed, and just the sound of his voice from out in the yard was enough to make tears blur my vision.

"Brody!" I screamed, running toward the sound of his voice. "He has a gun!"

I heard some sounds behind me. I knew Snake would be taking aim in mere seconds, but I kept on running, moving as fast as my feet would let me.

Brody appeared in the doorway, his face wild with fear and his eyes like huge dark saucers. When he saw me, he burst into action, rushing into the house, reaching for me.

So close.

He was just so close.

The last thing I saw was him literally throwing himself into the air at me.

The last sound I heard was the explosion of a gun.

23

Brody

Pulling up to the house and seeing the light from the inside spill out across the front porch from the open door was scary.

Hearing her scream my name shaved about ten years off my life.

All I knew was that something bad was happening, she was covered in something wet and sticky, and the fear on her face was one of the realest things I'd ever seen.

When Snake appeared in the hallway behind her, brandishing a gun, my heart nearly stopped in my chest. I was still too far away. It seemed like the distance between us was miles.

Snake lifted the gun and pulled the trigger.

I leapt, launching myself off the floor and jumping at her.

On my way down, I wrapped my arms around her body and rolled, trying to take the impact of the fall. We hit the side of the wall and slid down. I rolled, pinning her beneath me and lifting my arm, which was also brandishing a gun.

I squeezed off two shots in rapid succession, and then the room fell into absolute silence.

Only after I saw Snake lying on the ground, twitching, did I lower my weapon. But even still, I didn't trust him. I pushed off the floor and reached for Taylor, who was shaking uncontrollably. She was covered in something and it made me frantic.

"What happened?" I asked, running my hands all over her body, looking for bullet wounds. The shot Snake fired just moments before hit the wall just above us, but that didn't mean he hadn't shot her before I got here. "What the hell is all over you?"

"It's eggs," she said, a hysterical laugh bubbling up from her throat.

"Eggs?" I asked, glancing back at Snake, who was bleeding on the floor. He appeared to be unconscious, but I wouldn't believe that until I walked over there and kicked him.

"I was making you French toast." She laughed again, her body still shivering.

"Aww, Tay," I said, pulling her against me. The minute her face hit my chest, she started to cry. Deep, heaving sobs that wracked her body and made the inside of my gut shrivel.

"There's a big mess in the kitchen," she wailed, like that was somehow worse than almost dying for the third time in three days.

"I'll clean it up, baby," I told her, stroking my hand down the back of her head.

Snake groaned and Taylor shrieked, plastering herself even closer to me.

I wish I could say I was the bigger man. I wish I could say I knocked him out with a punch to the side of the head.

It wasn't good enough for me.

Instead, I shot him.

I made sure he was dead.

Taylor started to cry again, and I wrapped my arms around her and picked her up, sitting down on the steps and cradling her in my lap.

The first of several patrol cars pulled into the driveway, and I laid the gun down beside me. "It's over now," I told her, stroking her back. "He's dead and the rest of his buddies are in jail."

"What about you?" She sniffled.

"What about me?" I asked.

"How many others are going to come for you?"

It was something I couldn't bring myself to lie about. "I don't really know."

She buried her face in my neck and the wetness of her tears against my skin made me feel sick. "I was so scared," she whispered.

"Being attacked is scary." I agreed.

She jerked up, her wide, green eyes tearful. "I wasn't scared for me."

I frowned and wiped away one lone, fat tear making a track down her cheek. "What were you scared of, then?"

"I was scared he was going to shoot you," she said, her voice breaking on the last part as she started sobbing again.

All these tears were for me?

Cops started rushing inside, weapons drawn, all of them looking at me. "He's there," I said, motioning with my head as I tried to swallow back the emotion clogging my throat.

It'd been so long since someone worried about me.

"He's dead," I said, flat. "He tried to kill us."

Police started milling around as Mac entered the house.

His eyes widened when he took in Taylor, who was still wiping tears from her face. "What the hell happened, West?"

"The real Snake showed up."

"Any injuries?"

"Tay," I said gently. "How bad are you hurt?"

"I'm not," she replied, leaning her cheek against my shoulder.

"We're good." I glanced over at Snake's unmoving body. "He's not."

Mac nodded and went over to give some orders to the guys standing over Snake.

"Taylor," I said quietly, nudging her so she would look at me. Reluctantly, she pulled back and sat up. "This is really shitty timing. And I'm probably a big dick for doing this, but it's something I have to say."

"What?" Her eyes stayed dry and her limbs were no longer shaking.

"What happened here tonight... I can't promise it won't ever happen again." I couldn't help but run my palm over the side of her hair while I spoke. I was very aware that this might be the last time she let me hold her like this. "My career as an undercover cop is over, but I'm still a cop. If I stay here—if you still want me— there might always be that chance that someone will recognize me from my time in the organization. I can cover up that tattoo on my back, but the effects of it are permanent."

"Brody," she began, and I shook my head.

"Think about it, Tay. Think about what happened here tonight, what happened at the lake earlier today. Think about how scared you were. Being with me is a risk. I swear I will do everything humanly possible to protect you, and I really don't think I'll have any more problems with the organization, but I can't guarantee it."

I fell silent. I said everything I needed to say. I gave her an out and I would totally understand if she took it. Some things—*some people*—just weren't worth the risk.

"You're such an idiot."

I blinked, not sure I heard her right. "Excuse me?"

She sighed. "I said you're an idiot. A big, fat one." She wiggled her butt so it was more solidly in my lap and glared. "If you think I would allow some stupid pack of criminals to make me walk away from the first man in my entire life that actually made feel something special, then you, sir, are an idiot."

"A pack of criminals…" I echoed.

"You know you aren't the only one with a tattoo," she said, looking up at me through partially lowered lashes.

"You have a tattoo?" I asked, surprised. I had been over every inch of her body and I didn't see any tattoo.

She nodded. "You can't see it, but the effects of it are permanent."

I shook my head, still wracking my brain, trying to think about where it might be.

"You're the one who gave it to me," she whispered, picking up my hand and laying it against her chest. "It's right here," she murmured. "Right here on my heart."

"Tay," I whispered. It sounded more like a prayer, maybe because it was.

"Some people are just worth the risk."

A wall inside my chest, a wall I hadn't even realized was there, crumbled to pieces. I kissed her as if we weren't in the center of a crime scene full of people. It was the first kiss of the rest of my life.

Finally, I was home.

EPILOGUE

Taylor

It was the middle of the day, not quite lunchtime, but close. I parked just outside my townhouse and jumped out of the car, practically running up the walk toward the front door. The keys jangled as I riffled through them, looking for the one to unlock the door.

My hands were trembling with excitement and it was hard to think. I was still fumbling with the keys when the front door opened and a muscular, tattooed arm reached out and grabbed me, yanking me into the cool air-conditioned inside.

I giggled as the keys clattered onto the floor and the door slammed shut. Brody pounced, pushing me up against the back of the door and pinning me with his already rock-hard erection.

He was completely naked, and I squealed with satisfaction.

"You're late," he growled.

"Meeting." I gasped as he ripped open my shirt and buttons went flying in all directions. His hands were rough as he yanked down the lacey black cups of my bra, completely exposing my breasts.

He didn't say anything more as he dipped his head and drew one of the aching nipples into his mouth, sucking on it vigorously and making me cry out with pleasure. As he sucked, my arms wound their way around his back, and I dug my hands into the backs of his shoulders.

Brody rotated his hips and his straining cock poked at my abdomen, rocking against me... practically dry-humping against the wall. I reached between us and took his large member in my hand, squeezing around the head and making him shudder.

He ripped away his mouth and moved over to the next breast, where he began nipping at the sensitive flesh. The more I squeezed, the more he nipped.

I laughed a throaty laugh because he felt so incredibly good.

Finally, he lifted his head and moved upward, capturing my lips with his. I sighed into him as that completely intoxicating tongue of his swept deep inside my mouth. I purred when his hand went around behind me and slid down the zipper of my skirt.

I needed him so badly that I helped push away my skirt, discarding the panties right there beside the door with it. I'd learned a long time ago not to wear stockings. They ended up shredded in pieces on the floor.

I wrapped my arms around his shoulders and he lifted me. My legs wrapped around his hips and I pushed my already wet and ready center along his abs, the tight ridges of his muscles making my inner walls flex with need.

He took several steps backward and lowered himself on the stairs with me straddling his lap.

"Ride me," he growled, picking me up by the waist and centering me on his steely, unbending rod. I slid over him gladly, wrapping him in my sleek heat. My nails dug into his chest as he filled me to capacity, and his head fell back while he groaned loudly.

I leaned forward, licking up the center of his throat and trailing wet kisses over his flesh. He grabbed my hips and I started to move, riding him like he was a wild bull and I was a cowboy.

Every single time I rocked, the sides of his rigid length would rub along my inner walls, massaging the swollen, needy flesh and making me moan. Brody wrapped his arms around me and surged upward, angling his hips off the stair and penetrating me even deeper. I bore down on him. The pressure of our bodies rubbing together was so good that it made me cry out.

When his lips closed over my nipple and tugged, an orgasm ripped through me. I felt my wet insides coat him as his cock began to pulse within me. I kept rocking, unable to stop. The waves of pleasure just kept crashing over me.

Brody slammed himself up inside me one last time and shouted my name. His hot seed spilled inside me, and my body gulped it in like I was a dying man in need of a drink.

I collapsed against him, my skin slick with sweat and breathing heavily. God, he was so unbelievable satisfying. Sometimes I marveled at the fact we'd been together for almost an entire year, yet we still rushed home on our lunch hours just so we could be together.

He drew lazy circles over my lower back with his fingertip, and I reveled in the way his touch made me quiver.

"Damn, I love living here," he drawled, the satisfaction in his tone undeniable.

Not long after we started dating, my best friend moved out to take a job a few hours away, and since Brody always told me I was his home, he moved in.

"I love you," I told him.

His sigh was content when he lifted my boneless body off his chest so he could look into my face with his espresso stare. "I love you, Taylor." His voice was husky from our heated sex.

I was never going to get tired of hearing him say that. I collapsed once more against his bare chest and sighed.

"I was thinking," he said. "We should get out of town for a bit, just me and you."

I sat up and stared down at him, the red waves of my hair falling between us. "Is it work? Has someone made a threat against you?"

"No, Tay." He tucked the hair behind my ear. "Nothing like that. There hasn't been one hint of a threat or retaliation since that night Snake came to your dad's."

I blew out a breath. It seemed his past with the organization was definitely behind us and wasn't going to be a risk toward our future. "Then why do you want to leave town?"

He smiled. "There's this thing called vacation…"

I smiled. "Oooh, I like the sound of that."

"I'm thinking Hawaii. The sand, the water, you… me…" He gave me a suggestive look, reaching up to cover my breast with his palm.

[233]

"I like the way you're talking."

"I was also thinking maybe while we're there… you might marry me."

The world stopped. It was as if we were a movie and someone hit pause. Long, incredible seconds stretched by. And then I took a breath.

"You want to get married?" I whispered.

"I want to tie myself to you in every possible way." From somewhere, despite his naked body, he produced a small velvet box.

I took it and carefully lifted the lid.

Nestled in the velvet pillow was a ring I knew very well. A sob ripped from my throat.

"How did you—" my voice broke as I reached down to finger the gorgeous antique ring. It was my mother's wedding ring. My mother's mother wore it before she passed it on to my father to give it to her.

As a child, I used to sit and admire it, thinking how beautiful it was and how much my father must have loved her to give her something so sentimental. It was something I always would associate with my mother because she never took it off. In fact, she loved it so dearly I thought she was buried with it when she died.

"When I went to ask your father for his blessing, he gave it to me."

My eyes filled with tears. "You asked my father?"

Brody nodded. "I respect him. He loves you."

A tear escaped and rained down across my cheek. I couldn't stop staring at the ring. It was more stunning than even I recalled.

"I didn't realize he had this," I said, fingering the delicate gold band.

"He told me right before she died, your mother took it off and gave it to him. She made him promise

[234]

that when the time was right, he would make sure you had it and that you knew how much she loved you."

A sob caught in my throat as even more tears flooded my face.

I couldn't speak. I could barely breathe when he took the box from my hands and removed the ring. I continued to cry and make a mess of myself as he positioned the ring to slide it over my finger.

"What's your answer, Tay?"

"Yes," I said, the word barely even comprehensible through my sobs.

It slid over my knuckle with ease, fitting into place like my finger was exactly where it belonged. I stared down at the unconventional ring, my chest expanding with joy. It wasn't a diamond, but instead, the large square center stone was a blue-green tourmaline that reminded me of the ocean waves. On each side of the stone was a cluster of three seed pearls. It was all set in a delicate eighteen-carat gold band that lovingly held tight to the stones.

"Oh my God, Brody, you have no idea what this means to me."

He smiled and reached up to stroke my cheek, wiping away some of the tears. "I'm going to love you forever," he vowed.

And he did.

THE END

Taylor's Overnight Pumpkin French Toast Bake

INGREDIENTS

1 loaf of French bread (or any type of bread you have – I always use French bread. It's roughly 5-7 cups of bread, cubed.)

7 eggs

½ cup of pumpkin puree (canned works!)

2 cups of milk (I use almond milk. You can use what you prefer.)

1 tsp vanilla extract

1.5 tsp of ground cinnamon

Shake of ginger (I literally shake the spice canister over the bowl to add a little)

Shake of nutmeg (I literally shake the spice canister over the bowl to add a little)

Brown sugar for topping (3-4 tablespoons)

Taylor's Overnight Pumpkin French Toast Bake (cont.)

DIRECTIONS

Tear or cut the bread into chunks or bite-sized pieces. Place bread into a lightly greased 9x13 baking dish and set aside. In a mixing bowl, mix together the seven eggs, pumpkin, milk, vanilla, and spices.

Pour the egg mixture over the bread cubes. Then, using your hand, press down lightly on the bread to soak the mixture through. Once the bread is moist, cover the dish tightly with a lid or plastic wrap.

Refrigerate overnight.

In the morning (Good morning!) preheat your oven to 350 degrees.

Sprinkle the brown sugar over top of the French toast (Be as generous as you like).

Bake for 35-45 minutes.

Serve warm with syrup or honey drizzled over the top (I also put butter on mine)!

Enjoy!

AUTHOR'S NOTE

I cannot believe I am sitting here writing the author's note/acknowledgements for the eighth *Take it Off* novel. When I decided to give writing the New Adult genre a go and add in some of that sexy flare everyone seems to love so much, I was so nervous.

I remember bellyaching to my writing buddies Cameo Renae and Amber Garza about how hard writing something without paranormal was and how I thought everyone would be bored to tears by it all.

Now I have a hard time thinking about switching back to paranormal.

Don't worry… I will. The *Death Escorts* series will get finished—hopefully sometime this year.

I just really want to acknowledge all of you—the readers. When I first started writing this series, I really didn't think it would get the amount of reception it did. I mean, sure, I hoped, but I didn't really expect it. It's been so awesome to be able to write these fun, sexy stories and have so many of you enjoy them.

So thank you.

Let's see… What was happening with me as I was writing this book? Well, as many of you know, I live in the South, in North Carolina. Well, it has snowed like three times since I started this book. That's the most it's ever snowed here in one winter since I moved here five years ago.

So while I was writing this book, we had lots of snow days, lots of no school, and lots of time in the house. I think it pretty much is starting to make me crazy!

Ahhhhhhhhhhhhhhhhhhhhhhhh!

Okay, I feel better now.

[238]

Actually, as I sit here and type this, *Robocop* is playing on TV. I've never seen it before. It's very eighties. Ha-ha-ha. And can someone please tell me why the police officers wear those helmets? It's a little odd... LOL!

Oh, and we adopted a new cat. It literally just came right in my house. My husband saw it standing at the back door one night and it looks similar to my other cat, Pumpkin. So he opened up the door and told "Pumpkin" to get in the house. Only it wasn't Pumpkin.

It's like that TV commercial where the woman invites a raccoon inside to snuggle. I guess I should be glad it wasn't a raccoon. LOL.

Anyway, he realized his mistake and put it back outside, and the cat hung around for days (Yeah, I fed it. You would have too.), but then we got another snow and ice storm and I sort of invited him inside. So, yeah, we have a new cat. His name is Cinnamon. We call him Cinny. He doesn't have very good manners. We're working on it.

I know you are all just so enthralled by my randomness that is this note. I'll wrap it up.

Oh! I almost forgot! I have OFFICIAL news! Cambria Hebert Books is now an "official" business. It is now Cambria Hebert Books, LLC. You can see my snazzy new logo at the beginning of this book. The talented Regina Wamba of Mae I Design designed it.

Again, I have you readers to thank for picking up my books and reading. It's because of all of you I was able to turn my dream into a business.

Next up, I will be writing *Tryst*. I hope you all enjoyed *Tattoo,* and if you did, please consider leaving a review!

[239]

See you next book!
Cambria

Turn the page for a sneak peek of
TRYST,
the next *Take It Off* novel,
coming April 2014!

TRYST
Sneak Peek

Talie

I hadn't had sex in six months. *Six months.* I was practically a born-again virgin. I mean, seriously. They say when you get married, your sex life goes down the toilet, but I didn't know who "they" were, and I thought for sure my sex life wouldn't go downhill until I was some old lady.

I was not old.

And I kind of wanted to punch "they" in the face.

I'll blame my aggression on sexual frustration.

Weren't men supposed to be a bunch of horn-dogs? In my experience, they sure were. My husband and I used to have sex all the time, but it slowly began to dwindle and then it pretty much fell off the face of the earth.

But that was going to change. I was going to do something about it. The way I saw it, I could let my insides shrivel up from lack of pleasure, or I could take the bull by the horns (or penis).

Shriveling up did not sound so appealing so I took the afternoon off from work (no loss there) and decided to go home and set the stage for a night of getting it on. On my way, I stopped at the store and picked up some candles, a see-through hot-pink nightie, and some edible massage oil.

I let myself into the apartment and shut the door behind me. Just as I made it to the kitchen counter, I heard a sound.

A moan.

I set the bag on the counter, soundlessly, and cocked my head, listening. Another moan floated through the apartment, and I wrinkled my nose.

Had I left the TV on when I left for work this morning?

And if so, what the hell kind of daytime shows did they play these days?

I padded down the hallway, over the plush carpet, and stopped in front of my partially closed bedroom door.

The sounds of heavy breathing and the bouncing of a mattress were unmistakable.

I was really trying not to think bad thoughts.

Really.

But I mean… it smelled like sex out here. A deep, musky scent that clung to the air.

I laid my palm against the door and pushed it open, stepping slowly in the doorway.

It took me quite a few seconds to register what I was seeing. Shock rendered me motionless. All I could do was stand there and gape.

I hadn't left the TV on this morning.

And now I knew why my husband hadn't pleased me in the past six months.

He was too busy pleasing someone else. Someone who was *not* his wife.

They were so involved in the act that they didn't even know I was there. So I watched them. This was my house. That was my bed. And frankly, a part of me thought I was dreaming.

The white combed-cotton sheets that I had shopped for diligently where all wound around the legs of the couple in the center of the king-sized bed. The pillows I loving picked out were all skewed from the thrusting and movement going on, and the dark-gray comforter was half falling off the bed and onto the floor.

There was a woman sitting on top of my husband. Her hair was very long and thick, the color of chestnuts, and it waved down her back wildly like they'd been at the deed for a while already. As I stared, she pushed up off him and sat up, titling her head back and letting out a very loud moan as she moved over him, grinding her body against his.

I watched as my husband reached up and grabbed her breasts, giving them a little squeeze and grunting with pleasure.

Pain sliced through my belly.

How could he do this to me? How could he tell me he loved me, ask me to spend the rest of my life with him, and then bring another woman home and into our bed?

The pain I felt might have been incapacitating, but it didn't stay long enough. It was quickly replaced by anger. Hot, furious sparks ignited inside me and my feet began to move.

I walked farther into the room and stopped at the edge of the bed.

"Talie!" My husband gasped, shooting into a sitting position. The woman screwing my husband didn't slide off of him. Instead, she buried her face into his naked chest, like she was trying to hide.

It pissed me off.

I reached out and grabbed a handful of that thick, luxurious hair and yanked her backward. "Get the hell off my husband, you dirty ho."

She screeched as I pulled her back off his lap, revealing his proud member. I scowled and dumped her and her fake boobs on the floor.

"Talie, I can explain," he said, pulling the blanket up to cover his manhood. He was probably nervous I might grab it like I grabbed Barbie's hair.

I wasn't touching that thing ever again.

And really... was that like every idiot's favorite line? *I can explain.*

"You don't need to explain. My eyes work just fine," I snapped.

The girl scrambled up off the carpet and started gathering her clothes, which were tossed around my bedroom.

"I hope he satisfies you because he sure as hell never satisfied me," I spat.

Her eyes widened and Blake (my cheating husband) began to sputter.

"Shut up," I told him as I grabbed Barbie again and started towing her through the apartment toward the front door.

"I'm not dressed!" she screeched.

"What a shame."

I flung open the door and shoved her out. She stood there in the center of the hallway, clutching her clothes against her naked chest. Her eyes narrowed and a mean look crossed her face.

"He told me you never made him happy."

"You might wanna pay a visit to the surgeon who did your tits. They're lopsided." I slammed the door in her shocked face.

My chest was heaving and my hands were shaking when I turned around.

Blake was standing there, buttoning up a pair of black slacks. "Was that really necessary?"

At least he didn't try to come up with some stupid-ass excuse. There was no excuse for him. And there was no excuse for why I married him, why I stayed in a marriage that was clearly never going to make me happy.

I opened the door once more. Thankfully, Barbie had already run off.

"Get out."

He stared at me.

"I'm pretty sure I didn't stutter. I said get the hell out."

"This is my apartment too," he said, crossing his arms over his chest.

"Oh, you can have it," I replied calmly. "I'll be gone in two hours."

His arms dropped to his sides. "Where are you going to go?" Shock registered on his face, and I realized then that he didn't respect me. He probably never did. He knew he would get caught eventually, but he thought I would stay. He thought I would put up with it.

He didn't know me at all.

"It's none of your business. Now get out before I start to scream."

He came forward, stopping just in front of me. He reached up as if he were going to touch my face. I slapped his hand away. "I'll be gone in two hours."

Once he was in the hall, I slammed the door and threw the locks. I sagged against the white-painted wood and expelled a breath. I felt like I just ran a marathon. My chest squeezed tight, my stomach hurt, and every single limb on my body was heavy and exhausted.

Tears threatened behind my eyes and I sniffled. I glanced at the bag full of my romance supplies.

What a big, fat freaking joke.

I shoved away from the door, lifted my chin, and dashed away the unshed tears.

I could feel sorry for myself later.

Right now, I had to pack.

Cambria Hebert is the author of the young adult paranormal *Heven and Hell* series, the new adult *Death Escorts* series, and the new adult *Take it Off* series. She loves a caramel latte, hates math, and is afraid of chickens (yes, chickens). She went to college for a bachelor's degree, couldn't pick a major, and ended up with a degree in cosmetology. So rest assured her characters will always have good hair. She currently lives in North Carolina with her husband and children (both human and furry), where she is plotting her next book. You can find out more about Cambria and her work by visiting http://www.cambriahebert.com.

Cambria Hebert